Heavy Heart

Heavy Heart

Elizabeth Menzie

Elizabeth Menzie

CONTENTS

For Garnet. Thank you for always being a wonderful
friend and a continued support of my work.

Chapter 1

I stood in line and waited for my turn to punch in. The morning shifts were always the busiest, with the largest output of any production team. I adjusted my hair net under my company baseball cap and sighed. I wondered what was taking so long, it was just the scan of a badge and then we could get to work. I peered ahead of me but I couldn't tell what was happening.

The shift supervisor came down the line and greeted each of us one by one as he passed. I nodded to him but didn't say anything. I wasn't sure he even knew my name to be honest. We were all invisible cogs in the meat packing machine of Jersey Land Meats. I put my protective goggles on and waited for my turn to clock in. The line had started to move along finally, I was eager to get to work.

Once I scanned my badge I walked to my station. My job was monotonous; it was the same each day. Select the chicken wings, pack a dozen onto the styrofoam tray, put it on the conveyor belt which sends it down to be plastic wrapped for distribution. I stood on my anti-fatigue mat for several hours a day selecting the perfect wings for the trays. The rest of my day was spent cleaning up after each bucket of wings was gone through. In order to prevent cross-contamination we had to clean our stations down completely each time. Our attire had to be changed each time as well as our gloves. We also had to take the temperature of the meat every half hour, to ensure the proper cooling procedures were met.

I had been with Jersey Land Meats for eight years. I had gone to university right out of high school and worked very hard to get a degree in psychology. However, after I graduated I found it very difficult to find meaningful employment with just a Bachelor of Arts degree. I thought about going back for my Masters but I ran out of money. I found myself working at an all night gas station, alone and a little bit terrified.

I heard through the grape line in town that the meat packing plant was hiring entry level packers, so I applied. It wasn't hard to get on, all that was required was a grade twelve education and the ability to lift fifty pounds. That had been my life for eight years; clock in, work all day, clock out, go home, feed my cat, eat and go to sleep. My days were predictable, but there was a certain amount of comfort in it. I made decent money, I had full benefits and I was gaining a pension. Two years ago I finally had enough money saved up for the down payment on my little house on 7th Street. It wasn't fancy, but it had good bones, the furnace was new and the windows were only three years old when I bought it. I loved my house, it kept me busy.

I had started going through the tub of wings when my direct supervisor, Trevor Mattheson came up to me, "Layla, we have some overtime today. It's going to be about two hours after your shift ends, do you want it?"

I nodded, "Sure, why not." He smiled at me, "Thanks Layla, you are always willing to help out. I appreciate it." I smiled and returned to my work. I glanced at Trevor as he walked away. He was tall with sandy blonde hair and a goatee. He was happily married, but I'd always had a bit of a crush on him. Trevor was nice to me, he didn't make fun of me like some of the other guys did.

I went on with my day. After my overtime was done I clocked out and went to my locker. I changed out of my work coat and disposed of my hair net. As I left the ladies locker room there was a group of men outside in the lobby of the employee entrance. At the centre of it were my two least favorite co-workers; Brock Hansen and Zack Trulley. They had been in school with me from elementary all the way through grade twelve. We had been in the same class. My entire life, they had made fun of me because I was a bigger girl. Since we were all adults, you would think that childish behavior would be behind us; it wasn't. Brock and Zack both continued to call me the various pet names they had for me like 'the walrus' or 'the blob'. When I was a teenager it used to send me to the bathroom in tears, it would send me over the edge and cause me to want to hurt myself. Since I was older, I didn't let it get to me as much as I used to. I decided I wasn't going to let it tear me down, I was better then they were. I wasn't going to allow bullies to hurt me.

As I passed by the group of men, Brock shouted at me, "Hey Walrus, where are you going? Back to the sea?"

I rolled my eyes and ignored him. I found that not responding was the best way to deal with them. If I acknowledged their behaviour it only encouraged it. I just kept walking with my head held up high. I didn't care what they thought of me. I was a bigger girl and I wasn't going to allow their words to tear me down.

I went to the grocery store after work to pick up some dinner. I wasn't sure what I felt like, so I decided to pick up some pasta and sauce. I put a package of hamburger in my cart along with some mushrooms and green peppers. I needed cat food for Mr. Fuzz so I put a big bag at the bottom of my cart before I headed to the check-out. My best friend Jackie Newton was working. She was the head cashier at the Co-Op grocery store in our little community.

She smiled wide when she saw me; "Hey Layla, 2401 right?" I nodded.

"What's for supper tonight?" she asked me. I smiled, "Spaghetti and meat sauce with some veggies. I'm making lots so if you want you can come by after work.

Jackie shook her head, "Sorry, I work until 7pm tonight and then I have to head over to mom's house. She needs me to drain her dehumidifier in the basement. She won't go down there since she had the stroke."

I sighed, Jackie was one of the best people I knew. She took care of her widowed mother who had lost a great deal of her mobility when she had a stroke two years previous. Jackie went to her mom's place every day to make sure her mom took her medications. She made meals for her and brought them over every weekend so her mom would have lunches and suppers all week. We had been friends since high school, when Jackie and her mom had moved to our little town. Her mom and dad had gotten divorced, her mom moved from Edmonton to our community. Jackie and I became friends instantly, and we had talked to each other every single day since then, even when I was away at university.

"Do you want some help with meals this weekend?" I offered. Jackie smiled, "Yeah, that would be great. I'm going to make some pork chops and mushroom gravy, it's mom's favorite. Do you want to come over on Sunday morning? We could bake."

I nodded, "Yeah, that sounds awesome. Let's make scones! I've got homemade strawberry jam." As she scanned and bagged my groceries, Jackie said, "Sounds perfect. I can't wait. Maybe we will put in a bad chick flick." I shrugged but smiled.

I carried my bags out to my car and drove home. My orange tabby Mr. Fuzz greeted me in my front window. He was my three year old cat, he was demanding and adorable. He owned my heart and soul. I made my supper and ate it quietly. Mr. Fuzz cuddled up next to me on his chair while I ate. My life was simple and a little bit boring. I didn't mind it though, things were predictable and I knew what to expect. Little did I know that things were about to change.

Chapter 2

After work on Friday afternoon I went to the garden centre to pick out some plants for the flower pots in my backyard. It was the end of April, the perfect time to start putting in my flowers. I took a box and started walking around the greenhouse to see what was available. They had some lovely pansies in purple and gold, as well as snapdragons. I put six of each in my box and continued walking. My hand was holding a package of Miracle Grow when someone clears their throat behind me. I turned around to see Zack Truelly; he was also holding a box in his hands. I didn't make eye contact, I just stepped to the side so he could walk around me. I expected Zack to walk past me but instead he took a small step toward me.

I turned my back to him and continued down the aisle of plants. There were plenty of ways to get around me, I had left plenty of room for him. Zack shuffled toward me again, still not saying anything to me. I didn't meet his eyes when I asked, "Can I help you with something?"

"No, I was just trying to see what you are getting." he said quickly. I set my box down on the table and stepped away from it. I continued to look through the different kinds of plant fertilizers. When I didn't say anything to him, Zack attempted to continue the conversation, "Are those pansies?"

I nodded, still unwilling to look up. He sighed slightly before he asked, "Do you like purple and yellow?" I shrugged as I picked my box up and started to walk away. Before I could get very far, Zack was on my heels, "I think those are my mom's favorite. I'm here getting flowers for her actually for the front path in her yard. Do they have more of those?" I chose my box of plant fertilizer and set it in my tray. I pointed to the area where I got the pansies from and continued to walk away.

"Thanks Layla." he whispered before I got too far from him. My heart was pounding as I made my way to the checkout. I had no desire to engage in a conversation with Zack Trulley, he had been one of my tormentors for years. He and Brock used to take it upon themselves to insult me and hurt me on a regular basis, I had no interest in talking about plants with him. I had no interest in talking with him about anything.

While I waited in the lineup to pay for my bedding plants, Zack stepped up behind me. I rolled my eyes when he leaned over and made a casual comment about the waiting. He cleared his throat again and asked, "So, what are you doing this weekend, Layla? Anything fun?"

I shrugged and shook my head. Zack nodded and added, "I'm going to put in my mom's flowers tomorrow. She will love those pansies." I didn't reply. After I paid I went to my car and put my tray in the trunk. I climbed into my car as quickly as I could and pulled out of the parking lot. Zack came rushing out, he seemed disappointed to see me driving away. I glanced at him in my rearview mirror, only to sigh with relief that I didn't have to talk with him any longer.

I decided to put the plants in on Saturday morning, so I brought the plants in the house to keep them warm overnight. As I was making supper I got a text from my friend Sara, she wanted to go out that night. She had broken up with her boyfriend and wanted to have a girl's night out at the local bar. Though it wasn't really my thing to go out drinking, I decided it could be fun. I replied that I would meet her there by 8pm. After I ate some supper, I took a hot shower and started to get ready.

My hair was a natural blonde, I never had to dye it. I had hazel eyes and natural ruby red lips. I rarely wore make-up, but since we were going out I applied mascara and a touch of eyeliner. Nothing else. I picked out a longer purple shirt, pairing it with a thick black belt. I pulled on my black skinny jeans and black ankle boots. I blew out my hair and let it hang down, since I had to wear it pulled back for work it felt nice to have it down.

I stared at myself in my bathroom mirror as I brushed my teeth. I wasn't a small woman. I had spent many years of my adolescence hating my body. Both boys and girls had called me names and told me I was disgusting and gross. As I got older, I realized it said more about them then it did about me. By the time I was in grade twelve I began to love the skin I was in; the curves I had. My body was mine alone, and I refused to allow anyone to take that away from me.

By the time I was in university I was more comfortable with myself. There were a couple of guys I had dated, nothing serious. Though I was still technically a virgin, I had explored my sexuality quite extensively while I was away at school. The dating pool was pretty small in my home town though, I hadn't dated anyone from town since I'd moved back. Online dating was hit and miss, but I had my share of admirers. Getting dates wasn't hard, a relationship wasn't easy to find.

Sarah texted me that she was inviting a few others out to the bar with us. I sent her a thumbs up emoji before I put on some lip gloss. I stared at myself in the mirror, looking over the outfit I had put together. I was happy with it. As I turned off the bathroom light, grabbed my black clutch and headed out the door. It was party time with the girls.

Chapter 3

Sarah had invited a couple other girls we knew from high school; Lisa and Hannah. They were both two years younger than us, but it was a small town, we all knew each other. When I arrived the place was already full of people socializing and having a good time. I looked through the crowds for Sarah, finally finding her and the others at a corner table.

"There's my girl, Layla! We got shots coming." she announced as I sat down. Hannah and Lisa both laughed loudly.

I smiled and nodded, "Sounds good. I am going to the bar to get a beer." I left my clutch on the table and slipped my cash in my back pocket. Slowly I made my way to the bar and ordered a bottle of beer. As I waited I didn't notice someone had come up next to me and brushed their shoulder against mine. The sudden contact caused me to shift my eyes quickly to my left. Zack stood uncomfortably close to me, our shoulders touching, he was smiling down at me.

"Can I help you?" I asked dryly. He didn't seem phased by my tone, instead he smiled widely at me, "What are you drinking, Layla? Let me get you something." I shook my head and handed the bartender my cash, "No, I can buy my own drinks."

I walked away, leaving Zack standing there with his mouth open. I'd seen way too much of him that day. It was odd he continued to try and engage me in conversation. I had no idea what his motive was. As I rejoined my party, the shots had arrived. Each of us downed ours quickly before ordering another round.

Sarah took a long sip of her vodka and cranberry juice, she muttered, "I need to get laid. Are there any good looking guys here tonight?" Hannah laughed at her, "Sarah, you just broke up with Jack. Why don't you give it a bit of time before you get into something else."

"Who says I want to get into anything else serious? I just want to have some fun." Sarah whined. Lisa rolled her eyes and I laughed. Hannah sighed, "Actually, I could use something fun too. Maybe we should make a lap around the bar, see if there are any prospects?" Sarah nodded and took Hannah's hand, the two of them left Lisa and I behind.

"So, how are you?" Lisa asked me. I smiled, "I'm good. And you?" She shrugged. We didn't know each other particularly well, we only spent time together when our mutual friends got together. Lisa was watching something behind me. I turned around to see Zack looking in our direction. When he saw me look at him he turned away quickly.

Lisa smirked, "I think Zack Trulley is checking you out." I shook my head, "No he's not. Zack used to tease me about being fat in school all the time. He's not interested in me." She shook her head and leaned forward to whisper, "Things change. Maybe he's into you now." I frowned at her and hissed, "Well I'm not into bullies so he can stay the hell away from me." Lisa sat back in her chair and chuckled, "You need to let the high school shit go, Layla. People can change."

I didn't respond to her, but I glanced over my shoulder at Zack. I caught him looking at me again, this time he didn't look away. Instead he smiled at me. I didn't respond, instead I turned back to my table and chugged down the remainder of my beer. Lisa let out a cackle and shook her head at me. The waiter brought us another pair of shots, which we took down quickly.

Sarah and Hannah found their way back to us twenty minutes later. Sarah told us, "I ran into Brock and he wants us to join his friends at their table." I furrowed my brow and shook my head, "No way, I don't want to sit with those assholes."

Hannah let out a whine, "Come on, Layla, it will be fun. They aren't that bad." I glared at her, "Brock called me a walrus just three days ago as I was leaving work. He's an asshole." Lisa smiled and nodded, "I'll stay here with Layla. You two go and try to get picked up. I came here to hang out with the girls anyway. Layla and I can have a good time just the two of us." I smiled at her and nodded.

Sarah and Hannah linked arms and went over to the table where Brock and Zack sat with a bunch of other guys. I didn't watch them go, instead I just chuckled to myself.

"What's so funny?" Lisa asked. I sighed, "Girls will always ditch each other for guys. It's so pathetic. I should have known Sarah would blow me off once a man came along."

Lisa nodded slowly, "Yeah I hear you. Listen, head's up, Zack is coming over here right now." My entire body tensed up. I held on to my beer bottle as tight as I could. I felt a breeze of movement pass by me as he stepped up next to me. I didn't make eye contact yet again, I just waited for him to speak.

Zack placed a beer bottle in front of me on the table, "Here, I bought you a drink. Will you consider coming and joining our table?" I shook my head. Lisa snickered at him. I glared at her but it didn't seem to phase her. Zack let out a sigh, "Layla, come and hang out with us. It will be fun."

I'd had enough of his weird behavior. Zack had been paying entirely too much attention to me and I'd had enough of it. I stood up and met his gaze. Zack looked into my face and smiled, I sucked in a deep breath before I spoke, "Listen, I don't know what you are playing at but I'm not interested. I'm not an easy lay, so stop trying. I don't need nor do I want your attention, Zack. So take your drink and shove it up your ass. Three days ago you and your buddy were making fun of me at work so don't think that just because you showed me a little attention all is for-given."

He stared back at me, his eyes wide and his mouth open. I crossed my arms over my chest and waited for him to respond. After a moment Zack swallowed hard, "I'm sorry, Layla. I should have said something when Brock made fun of you. You know it's all in good fun, he doesn't mean it."

I glared at him, "Really? Making fun of my body is fun for you? Is insulting me a joke? Tell me how that is supposed to make me feel good about hanging out with you, Zack?" He tried and failed to form words, instead he stood there with his mouth open and stared at me.

"You can go now. Take your beer with you." I hissed. Zack took the bottle from the table and retreated back to his friends. Lisa let out a hard laugh as I sat back down in my chair. I was proud of myself for standing my ground and coming to my own defence. I wasn't going to let some annoying man lure me into his bed. I wasn't interested in a one night stand or being used by Zack Trulley. He could stay far away from me.

Lisa and I spent the rest of the night together drinking beer and exchanging stories. Hannah came back to our table a few hours later. Sarah ended up going home with some random guy none of us really knew but she insisted she was fine. Hannah's sister came to pick us up from the bar at closing time. Before we left Zack tried to talk to me again but I closed the door in his face before he could say anything. I couldn't figure out why he kept trying to talk to me when I had made it clear I wasn't going to let him take me home. I'd already made my feelings about him known, yet Zack kept trying to come over to me. I had no idea what he was playing at, but I didn't want to bother spending a bunch of time on him. Once a bully, always a bully right?

Chapter 4

I spent all of Sunday with Jackie at her place. We made scones and muffins in the morning. It was always fun to have cooking days with her. We'd been friends for a long time, I considered Jackie my best friend.

"So have you been to the greenhouse yet?" she asked me as she pulled the pork chops out of the fridge.

I nodded, "Yeah, I picked out pansies and snapdragons for my pots this year. I planted them yesterday, they look pretty nice. You will have to come over for drinks some night this week and we can sit out back, maybe light a fire."

Jackie smiled, "That sounds great. I was going to plant some things for my mom this year, but I don't think I'll have time. I barely have time to keep her alive." I offered her a caring smile, "Maybe it's time to think about homecare."

She shook her head, "We can't afford private homecare and she doesn't need full time anyway. I'm trying to convince her to move in with me. Then we could sell her house and that would take care of any extra expenses while I'm at work." I nodded, encouraging her to continue. Jackie let out a sigh, "However, she doesn't want to give up her independence yet. My mom wants to stay in her own house, on her terms."

I was chopping mushrooms and putting them into a bowl for the mushroom gravy. I paused for a moment and looked at her, "That kind of puts you in a rough spot though." She chuckled, "Tell me about it. She's stubborn, but it's her life. She's not so bad that I worry about her survival or anything but I just can't imagine she's comfortable."

I shrugged, "It's hard to give up your own space when you've had it for so long. They say growing old is not for the faint of heart." Jackie nodded, silently agreeing with me.

"I don't mind helping out with your mom, you know. Anything you need and I will be there. I can cook for her, clean on the weekends, doctor's appointments. Whatever." I offered. Jackie smiled at me, "That's Layla. I appreciate that. Honestly, I do ask you when I need help. Thanks."

I didn't have any family left. My dad had a heart attack when I was eight and my mom passed away four years after I graduated from high school. There wasn't much left for me in our little town, but I had inherited property and land from my mother. There were two sections of farm land which I rented out to a local farmer, which brought in a decent amount of income for me. I'd also inherited my family's home in town, which I sold to buy the smaller house I currently lived in. It wasn't so bad to be twenty-seven and debt free.

I cleared my throat before I spoke to Jackie, "You know, if you want, I could help you with the homecare. I've got the funds." She shook her head, "No, I don't want to take money from you. You do enough for us already, Layla. Thank you though." I nodded and dropped the subject. Money was a hard topic for Jackie. She knew I could afford it, but she was proud. I understood it.

We spent the day talking about life in general. She'd been dating a guy in the next town over for about six months. I'd met him, he seemed nice but he was nothing special. As we were packaging up the pork chops into single serve containers Jackie said, "He's alright, kind of boring though. It's not that I don't like Casey, but he has no ambition. He just wants to come over to my place, watch TV and have sex. He doesn't want to do anything with his life beyond working at the tire shop. I don't know, Casey is just... meh."

I laughed at her description, "It sounds like you are just using Casey as a seat filler until you find someone else." I told her. Jackie shrugged, "Maybe I am. He's a nice guy, honestly he is. He just doesn't say much. He does whatever I want to do, whatever I suggest. His family is nice. I don't know, maybe I'm just trying to find something wrong with him."

"If you aren't feeling it, you can't force it." I offered. She nodded, "True. Anyway, what about you, Layla? Anyone interested?" I shook my head, "No, no one at the moment." She nodded and continued ranting about how boring Casey was. I half listened as I thought about Friday night at the bar with my friends. I thought about how weird Zack had been. I was dreading going to work the next morning in case he decided to be mean. I'd already promised myself if that happened I would go to human resources but I didn't want to have to do that.

Jackie and I had made some pasta and sauce for ourselves before I went home after supper. I fed Mr. Fuzz and watched some reruns of CSI: Miami. After a couple of episodes I went to bed and sent up a silent prayer that Zack wouldn't be rude to me the next morning at work. I didn't want a repeat of highschool bull-shit, I was too old for that.

Chapter 5

The meat packaging plant was in full swing by the time I got to work. I clocked in quickly and went to my station. We had big orders to fill so Trevor was making his rounds reminding us to go as fast as possible while still maintaining safety standards. I think there was going to be overtime that day, which didn't matter to me. I'd happily do some more overtime, it all went into a separate savings account I had made for a trip to Mexico. I just tuned out the sounds around me and kept putting my chicken wings in the trays.

When the lunch bell rang I grabbed my bag from the cooler and went to the break room. I sat with Lisa and Hannah, who were already talking about Sarah's weekend hook-up. Hannah wrinkled her nose as she ate her sandwich, "I can't believe she went home with a guy she didn't know. He could have any-thing."

Lisa chuckled, "You are such a prude, Hannah. Like you never slept with a guy you didn't know." Hannah looked at her with a horrified expression on her face, "I haven't! That is dirty!"

I filled my face with my wrap to keep from smiling too wide at their exchange. Hannah frowned at Lisa, "I've never done that, nor would I ever. It's gross. That's how rumors get started, Lisa!"

"What does it matter who she sleeps with? It's none of our business." I muttered. Lisa nodded as she opened her fruit cup, "Exactly. It's our job as her friends to take her to the clinic when she gets hepatitis." Hannah gagged, which caused Lisa to unleash a loud cackle. I shook my head and giggled.

Lisa, who was sitting across from me, let her smile fall as her eyes focused on someone standing behind me. I turned to see Zack there, holding his lunch bag in one hand, his hand rubbing his neck awkwardly with the other, "Good afternoon ladies, would you mind if I joined you."

"Yes we would." I said matter-of-factly. Hannah cleared her throat while Lisa just stared at him. Zack's face turned red, "It's just lunch, Layla. There is nowhere else to sit."

I looked around the break room and noticed Brock had an empty seat next to him three tables away. I pointed to it, "I think your bestfriend is saving you a seat." Zack looked away, then back to me, "I'm sorry about Friday alright. Can I just join you, please?"

I frowned at him and muttered, "Why do you want to sit with us, Zack?" He didn't answer, he just shuffled his feet side to side and stared at the ground. Lisa took pity on him and offered Zack her seat, she stood up, "Come on Hannah, we need to go to the bathroom." Hannah let Lisa pull her way from our table. Zack looked nervous as he opened up his bag and took out two sandwiches and opened up the plastic wrap carefully. We sat together in silence. I nibbled on my carrot sticks and scrolled through my phone.

"So, how was your weekend?" Zack asked me. I glared at him, "What are you up to? Seriously? What do you want?" He sighed and set his sandwich down, "I have been trying to apologize for Friday but you won't let me. I want to say that I should have said something to Brock when it happened."

I took out my scone and broke off a piece, "So what makes Friday so special? You and your friends have been making fun of my weight since elementary school. Brock and you used to steal my pudding cups and tell me I was too fat to have them. You used to push me into my locker in high school and tell me it didn't hurt because I had enough extra padding. Nothing was special about Friday, it was tame compared to what you two used to say to me when we were younger."

Zack looked at me, he seemed to be embarrassed by his own behaviour. I let my words hang in the air around us for a few moments before I continued, "Look, if it makes you feel better then it's fine. I'm over what Brock said on Friday. Whatever. Now, will you just leave me alone?" He looked saddened by my request, he muttered, "I forgot I pushed you into the lockers. That was mean."

I chuckled, "No shit it was mean. I was there, I remember it well." Zack sighed and shook his head, "I'm sorry, Layla." I rolled my eyes, "Ok, fine. Thanks. Are we done now?" He didn't say anything, he just looked into my eyes and forced a sad smile.

I was so preoccupied with Zack's apologizing, I hadn't noticed Brock came up next to him at the table, "Hey man, why are you sitting with the walrus? Did you not pack enough lunch so you need some of hers? Remember how we used to liberate your desserts in elementary school? Say, what do you have in there today?" Brock reached his hand over to my scone and tried to take it but Brock grabbed his hand and roughly pushed it away, "Leave Layla alone. I think we've done enough for her over the years."

"Is that your name? It doesn't suit you, it's too pretty." Brock shot at me. I glared at him, "You know, Brock, for a guy who thinks so highly of himself you spend a lot of time trying to knock me down. Perhaps you need a hobby." He muttered something unkind and turned to Zack, "So, are you coming outside with me for a walk or are you staying here with the blob?"

Zack frowned at his friend and shook his head, "Her name is Layla, and I'm staying here. You don't have to be such a dick to her, you know." Brock scoffed, turned his back and shuffled out of the break room. I continued to eat my scone and not make eye contact with the man across the table from me.

"You don't deserve that. I'm sorry." he whispered. I shrugged but didn't look up, "It doesn't matter. I'm used to being treated like a second class citizen by guys like you." Zack cleared his throat, "I'm not like him, Layla."

I rolled my eyes and sighed, "Alright Zack, sure you aren't. Whatever makes you sleep at night. I'm going back to work, see you later." As I stood up he caught my wrist, "Listen, um, would you like to go out with me sometime?"

"Huh?" I asked. I wasn't sure I heard him correctly. Zack sighed, "Would you like to go to dinner with me tonight?" I stared at him for a moment, "I think I'll pass. See you around, Zack."

I pulled my wrist from his grasp and moved toward the doorway. I could feel his eyes on me as I walked. As I left the room I exhaled a breath I had been holding. Hannah and Lisa were nowhere to be found, so I made my way to my locker then back to my workstation to finish the orders we had for the day. Just as I had suspected there was going to be overtime, I was pleased, it meant more cash in my Mexico account.

Chapter 6

By the time it was 6pm I had finally clocked out. Four hours of overtime wasn't too bad, though I had to admit I was tired. Hannah and Lisa had refused it so they left at their usual time. There were only about ten of us women who had stayed for it. As I walked through the locker room and out to the lobby I found Zack was waiting for me. I frowned when I saw his face but he was not deterred. He walked up to me and smiled, "Hey, I was hoping I would catch you before you took off for the day."

I crossed my arms over my chest, "Zack, I think I've been pretty clear that I don't want anything to do with you so what you are doing is boarding on harassment. So, just leave me alone." He took a step back, his eyes wide, "I just want to talk to you, I'm sorry if I'm coming on too strong. I want to make things right."

I laughed dryly, "There is nothing to make right. You bullied me when we were kids and now you feel bad about it. You are trying to clear your conscience or something. It's fine, I'm over it. I don't want anything from you so just have a nice life." I moved past him and walked out the front door. The sun was starting to sneak down the skyline as I crossed the parking lot to my car.

Zack's hurried footsteps came up behind me, "Layla, look, I want you to go out with me. A real date, I want to get to know you." I spun around and glared at him. He froze in his tracks, almost knocking me over. As his body made contact with me I let out a small grunt, "So you want a date? With me? In public?"

He moved away and nodded, "Yes. That's what I want. Let me take you out. We could go for supper and then a walk or something." I sighed, "Why?" Zack cocked his head to the side, "Because I think you are cool and I want to get to know you better."

"So you are looking for a booty call?" I snapped. Zack shook his head, "No! I just want to take a pretty girl I like out on a date. Why is that so suspicious?" I frowned, "It's suspicious because you spent our childhoods picking on me for being undesirable. You have to know I find it difficult to believe a single thing you say when that history is what I have to go on. People don't just change overnight."

Zack scoffed and ran his hand through his dark black hair, "Layla, I have to tell you, I always liked you. From like grade one, I thought you were so pretty, I always wanted to be your friend but with the cliques in highschool we may as well have been from two different worlds." I set my fists on my hips and bit my lower lip, "Oh really? So instead of being civil you pushed me into lockers everyday? That's so immature, the whole boy picks on the girl he likes theory. It's pathetic, Zack."

"I don't have a good excuse,I know I treated you badly when we were kids. I'm trying to apologize, I know it will never make up for it but I am very sorry for how I was to you. If I could take it back I would. All I'm asking for is a chance. Let me show you I can be good to you." he begged. I sighed and shook my head, "I'm not going on a date with you, Zack. So forget about it. I'm not going to give you the satisfaction of standing me up some-where."

He sighed and nodded, "Ok, I deserved that. I was hoping enough time had passed that maybe you could forgive me. I guess not, but I'll respect that." Zack turned and started to walk away. I don't know what possessed me to say it but I called after him, "But, if you want to sit with me at lunch time and eat that would be ok."

He stopped in his tracks and looked back at me, he smiled, "Ok, I'll see you tomorrow." I nodded and turned back to my car. I watched Zack climb into the cab of his truck through my rear view mirror. He was smiling to himself and he did a little 'yes' gesture before he pulled out of the parking lot. I shook my head and pulled out of the parking lot after him to drive home. Mr. Fuzz greeted me at the door, demanding wet food and treats. I chuckled at my demanding feline companion as I set my things down next to the door.

After I fed my cat and ate supper I called Jackie to see how her mom was doing. We had a short visit as she had to go, her mom was having a particularly rough day. She had to miss work that day because of it. I told her I would bring over some home-made soup tomorrow after work. She was grateful for my ges-ture, I told her I would help her as much as I could. I wished she would just take the money I offered, I had more than enough and I would love to help her out. She was too proud for that though, at least for now.

The next day Zack joined me for lunch just like I had offered. Hannah and Lisa joined the table as well. They kept looking at me with suggestive eyes but I ignored their immaturity. Zack spent most of the lunch hour talking with my friends instead of me, possibly because I wasn't making a conversation between the two of us easy. From the corner of my eye I noticed Brock was at his usual table alone. It seemed that without Zack to eat with, no one else wanted to join him. There was a brief moment of satisfaction in that before I felt empathy for him.

"So, Layla, what are you doing after work today?" Zack asked me. I took out my fruit cup and opened it up, "I am making some soup for Jackie Wattash's mother. I've got to go to the Co-Op after work and pick up some stuff for it."

He pursed his lips for a moment, "That's nice of you to do." I shrugged, "She's a good friend of mine and her mom had a stroke last year. It's been hard on both of them because her mom can't take good care of herself anymore."

Hannah smiled, "Layla is a very good person, you know. When I had a terrible flu she bought me groceries and picked up my prescriptions." Lisa chuckled and teased, "Bitch, you've never done anything nice for me!" I smiled at her and giggled,

"Well maybe it's because you always refer to me as 'bitch'." Lisa laughed out loud and nodded, "Ok, point taken."

"Anyway, I'm going to make homemade potato bacon soup for her. It will help out Jackie a great deal. We usually do some meal preparations together on the weekends for her mom but this week she just needs a little extra help." I told him. Zack didn't say anything but I could tell he was touched by my actions. He continued to eat his lunch with us, exchanging little antidotes with Hannah and Lisa. It wasn't awkward, it was easy.

The rest of the week was just like that. Everyday at lunch time Zack would join our table and eat with us. He would make casual conversation with Hannah and Lisa but always attempted to engage with me more. I didn't make it easy for him, but I had to admit I was warming up to him. Zack was a nice guy, I had learned. He had a good sense of humor and he liked to talk. I was surprised to learn I actually enjoyed his company.

Chapter 7

Jackie and I got together at my house on Saturday. I could tell she was exhausted. As I poured her a cup of coffee, I asked her, "How's it going?" She forced a hard laugh, "I had to miss three days of work this week because my mom kept having accidents in bed. She would freak out and then hit me because she was embarrassed and upset. It was terrible."

I sighed and passed the mug to her. I walked around behind her and pulled her into a hug. Jackie leaned back into my arms and sighed, "I don't have any more sick time that I can take so I had to take unpaid time off. My boss is understanding about it, but she can't pay me for my missed days." I tightened my grip around her shoulders and nodded silently, I was trying to offer her comfort and it seemed to be working.

"I'm really scared, Layla. I don't know what else to do, I think I'm losing my grip." she whispered. I nodded silently and held her as tears started to stream down her face. Jackie let the light tears turn into deep sobs. She let go of all the hard emotions she had been holding on to for a while. She was completely overwhelmed, trying to hold everything together for her mom. I stood behind her, holding on to her while she cried for almost an hour.

After a while I let her go and went to my cupboard where I keep my cheque books. I found the one for my Mexico account and I took it out. As I sat back down at the table next to Jackie, I said, "Listen, I know you don't want it but I'm giving you some money. You need the help, and having a cushion is going to make a difference. Especially if you have to miss work."

I filled out the cheque for five thousand dollars, which was almost the entire amount in that account. When I passed it to Jackie, her eyes went wide when she saw the amount, "Layla, I can't accept this. It's too much." I shook my head and pushed it into her hand, "No, you need it more than I do. This is my extra fun account, so I don't care about it. Take the money and hire some help. When it runs out let me know and I will give you more."

Jackie took the cheque and held it in her hands, "How can I accept more? You help me out so much already." I smiled, "Because you and I are like family. Family takes care of each other. You need my help and that is what family does, we help each other out." She took my hand and squeezed it tight, "Thank you, I don't know what else to say."

I shook my head, "Nothing else to say. Just take it. Tell me when you need more and I'll help you out." She sighed, "I think my mom is convinced that it's time to move in with me. She doesn't want to live alone anymore so that will help a lot. Once she moves in with me I can sell her house and that will open up a lot of money for extra care." I smiled and nodded.

"When do you think that move would happen?" I asked her. Jackie bit her lower lip, thinking for a moment, "Probably in about a month. I'll need to clean the house out, she won't be able to do much of the heavy stuff." I chuckled, "I think I can get some extra hands to help out. Lisa and Hannah would help for sure and I know a couple of guys with trucks."

Jackie nodded, she wasn't really listening to me. There was so much on her mind, I couldn't blame her. We spend the majority of the day making food and discussing her future plans for her mom. It wasn't easy for her, trying to plan out what to do when the roles between a parent and a child get reversed. She wanted her mom to maintain her autonomy as much as possible. It was important to her, therefore it was important to me.

Lisa texted me late in the afternoon asking if I wanted to join her and Sarah at the bar that evening. I agreed to go, I asked Jackie if she was interested in coming too. She shook her head, "I can't really go out. Thanks for asking though." I felt a bit guilty, because all her time was spent with her mom. Jackie never had any time for herself, and when she did it was doing meal preparations or working. I hoped once they had some homecare help she would be able to do a few more things just for herself.

I agreed to meet the girls around 9pm at the bar. Jackie left just before supper time. I warmed up some leftovers and watched a movie. At 7pm my phone went off, it was Hannah. She said that Zack asked her for my number and she wanted to know if it was alright to give it to him. I agreed reluctantly but I figured it wouldn't do any harm. A few minutes after I responded to her text I got a phone call from a number I didn't recognize. I knew it was him.

"Hello?" I asked as I answered the phone. Zack cleared his throat before he spoke, "Hey Layla, I got your number from Hannah. I hope you don't mind." I sighed, "So, what's up Zack? What do you want?"

He went quiet for a moment before he cleared his throat again, something I noticed he did when he was nervous, "I was just wondering what you were up to tonight?" I frowned and told him, "Well if you would like a play by play I am currently eating leftovers and watching a movie. I'm going out with my friends later."

"That's cool, what movie?" he asked. I sighed, "Face Off." Zack chuckled, "That's an old one, wow. Is it on VHS?" I snickered, "No, I have it on DVD. I like Nicolas Cage alright."

I could hear the smile in Zack's voice as he said, "He's pretty good. I liked him in Ghost Rider. Also National Treasure. Good movies." I rolled my eyes and sighed impatiently, "So did you call me just to get the play by play of my evening or did you actually have a reason for this silliness?"

Zack sucked in a deep breath before he spoke, "I was wondering if it would be alright if I joined you girls at the bar tonight?" I let the phone line go silent. I was sure Hannah had mentioned to him that we were going out when he asked for my number. I thought about it for a moment, he was asking to join with my friends, he wasn't asking me out directly. We would be in a group so it was just like the work lunches, I whispered, "Ok, sure."

"Cool, I'll see you there, Layla." he whispered, I could hear the smile in his voice. I hung up quickly before I could say anything else. I was suddenly very nervous. Zack Trulley was making me nervous. I stood up and walked around my living room, my stomach was in knots and my palms were sweating. I didn't like feeling so nervous. How could a silly thing like Zack calling me make me so nervous, I disliked that he was getting under my skin. I forced myself to take several deep breaths. It wasn't like he was the first guy to show any interest in me, and I refused to allow the small amount of attention he gave me to cloud my mind. I was stronger than that.

I looked at my reflection in my bathroom mirror. I muttered to myself, "Layla, come on, you are better than this. All he's after is sex so don't let it get to you. Once he gets what he wants, he'll be gone so get your head in the game." Zack may seem interested, but I reminded myself that guys like him were not what they seemed. There was always an ulterior motive, and I was not going to fall for it.

Chapter 8

I arrived at the bar by 10pm. I found Hannah and Lisa were already sitting with Zack when I arrived. I had purposely arrived later in the hopes that he wouldn't be there by the time I got there. I figured he would give up after a while and just go somewhere else or pair up with one of my friends when it took me too long to get there. Unfortunately, my plan didn't work. Zack had waited patiently for me to arrive, chatting politely with my friends. When they saw me come through the door Lisa shouted, "Layla, where the hell have you been bitch!"

I laughed out loud and crossed the room to the table, "Sorry, I was running late." Zack stood up and pulled out a chair for me to sit down, "I was beginning to think you stood me up." I frowned at him as I sat down, "This isn't a date, Zack. I never agreed to go on a date with you tonight so I can't stand you up if there isn't a date." Hannah let out a whistle and Lisa groaned, "Shut down man, bad luck."

Zack leaned over to me, "Would you like a drink?" I shrugged, not answering him. He took a step back and headed over to the bar. Lisa leaned across the table to me, "You know, I'm pretty sure that guy is into you. It might be time to be a little nicer to him."

I scoffed, "He's just looking to fuck and run. I'm not going to give him that." Hannah shook her head, "I don't think so, Layla. He's been sitting here for the last hour asking us how to get into your good books. I think he's actually into you."

"Whatever. Zack and Brock used to be so mean to me when we were growing up. I don't buy it, I'm surprised you two are." I hissed at them. Lisa chuckled, "Layla, listen to yourself. How long ago was highschool and you are still holding onto that? Everyone was an asshole in highschool. I'm still an asshole." Hannah and I chuckled.

"Where is Sarah? I thought she was supposed to be joining us?" I asked. Lisa shook her head, "She's out with that guy again. She said she might come by later in the night. I think his name is Dan, Dave, Don... she told me but I don't remember." I giggled and nodded.

Hannah leaned closer to me and said, "I think Zack has liked you for a lot longer than you think. He seems sincere. I think you should cut him some slack and give him a real chance." Lisa nodded and lifted her bottle of beer, "I agree!" I set my purse on the table and sighed, they had turned against me.

Zack came back with a full tray. He'd bought us all a round of beers and two shots each. I looked at the tray and smiled, "What did you get?" He smiled back at me, "I got us each a B-52 and an Orgasm." Lisa howled and said, "It's been a while since a guy gave me an Orgasm, thanks Zack."

He blushed and looked down, handing out the drinks to our table. I shot the B-52 down quickly followed by the Orgasm shot. They were delicious, I had to admit. Hannah took her shots with some difficulty, "Thanks Zack, I'm not much for shots but I'm trying." As I sipped my beer I giggled, "Yeah, thanks, Zack. It's my turn to buy shots next." He poured the drinks down his throat in one go, sat back and nodded.

We took turns telling stories and buying drinks throughout the night. I had to admit I was having a good time. By the time midnight rolled around, Zack's phone started to go off. He frowned when he opened his text message and set his phone on the table. I asked, "What's up? Do you need to go?" He shook his head, "No, it's just Brock. He's wondering where I am. He just wants to hang out."

I nodded, "Does he want to come here and join us?" Hannah and Lisa set their drinks down and stared at me. Zack looked at me with cautious eyes, "I don't know if that's a good idea, Layla. I can't guarantee what he will say if he joins us. Brock tends to run his mouth, he thinks he's being funny and he takes things too far."

"I think I can handle myself. If your friend wants to join us, tell him he can." I told him. Zack smiled at me and nodded, he sent a text message. A few moments later Brock came running into the bar. It was like he had been waiting for the invitation. Brock crossed the room to join our table and smirked at me, "I had to see this for myself, Zack out with you."

"Listen man, if you aren't going to act right, then go back home. I don't want to hear any of your shit." Zack hissed. Brock looked at his buddy then back to me, "Whatever. I need a drink." He stood up and went to the bar. I shifted my weight in my chair, wondering if it was such a good idea to include Brock.

Lisa leaned across the table, "If that asshat gets out of line, I'll kick his ass, Layla. Don't you worry." I laughed out loud and shook my head. Hannah nodded in her own sheepish way agreeing to put Brock in his place. "I'm a big girl, I can take care of myself. Don't worry about it. It was my idea to invite him anyway." I reminded them.

Hannah shrugged while Lisa sipped her beer. Zack leaned over to whisper in my ear, "Do you want to dance?" I looked out at the floor, there were three other couples out there slow dancing to a George Strait song. Without meeting his eyes, I nodded and stood up slowly. I let Zack take my hand and pull me onto the floor. He gently intertwined our fingers and pulled my hip close to his body with his other hand. I let out an involuntary gasp as his arm snaked around my torso to rest his other hand on my lower back.

I stared over his left shoulder, attempting to avoid eye contact. Zack started to sway with me around the dance floor. He whispered in my ear, "Are you nervous?" My eyes squeezed shut and I groaned, "No, not at all." He chuckled, his warm breath flowing over my neck, "Lier. I can tell you are nervous. Why are your eyes closed?"

"I'm just enjoying the song." I muttered. Zack slowly moved me around the floor. When the song was over I tried to move away but he held on to me. I raised my eyes to meet him, he smiled at me, "One more song, Layla." I sucked in a deep breath and nodded. I could feel my palm in the hand he was holding getting sweaty. I tried to break our eye contact but I couldn't look away from him. As a Garth Brooks song played I let Zack pull me even closer, resting both his arms around my torso. I set my hands on his shoulders and held on a little too tight.

I heard Lisa let out a whistle from our table but I couldn't break the gaze I had with Zack. He smiled at me, not saying a word. His eyes were full of emotions I couldn't read. I was sure I looked similar to a deer in headlights. The song seemed to go on forever, I started to feel light headed. Zack leaned down slightly and rested his forehead against mine. I exhaled a breath I'd been holding and leaned against him. He snickered, "See, I'm not so bad am I?" I shook my head against his but said nothing.

When the song ended I tried to pull away but he held on to me. I looked up at him, he whispered, "Don't run away on me. Let's walk back together." I sighed and nodded. I let him hold my hand and walk me back to the table. Zack pulled the chair out for me and sat down next to me. Everyone stared at us, I could feel my cheeks flush under their gaze.

"So are you two dating now?" Brock broke the silence with somewhat of a sneer. Zack shot him a look before answering, "What if we are? You got a problem with that, man?"

I cleared my throat, "We are not dating, we are friends, Zack. Just friends." Brock chuckled and sipped his beer, "Doesn't look like friends. Whatever, do what you want." Lisa and Hannah glared at him. I was surprised it was Hannah who actually spoke, "What's your problem with Layla anyway? It seems like you go out of your way to be rude to her for absolutely no reason."

Brock's mouth fell open, it seemed he wasn't expecting Hannah's blunt questions either. I smiled and sipped my beer quietly while we all waited for him to answer. After he scratched the back of his neck, he muttered, "I don't know. I've always given her a hard time, it's all in good fun." Hannah shook her head, "No, that's not good enough anymore. We haven't been kids for a long time, so that doesn't cut it anymore. You know that girls don't like bullies anymore right? It's not sexy to hurt other people."

Lisa wrapped her arm around Hannah's shoulders and chuckled, "That's my girl right there. You tell him!" Hannah blushed and leaned away, "I'm not trying to be mean, Brock, I'm just saying that it's immature to hold on to highschool stuff when it was so long ago. I think it's time to grow up." Brock stared at her, this tiny little mild mannered woman who was putting him in his place. I'd never seen Hannah so fearless in my life.

Brock looked down at his beer bottle and shrugged, "Alright, I can take a hint. I'll go now." Hannah stood up from the table before he could and grabbed his hand, "No, you should stay and have a good time. Just don't be a dick!" She pulled him out to the dance floor and forced him to dance with her to a Taylor Swift song. Brock looked like he had been hit by a truck, he was so shocked. The rest of us just watched as Hannah danced around the floor with him, a huge grin on her face.

"Did someone give her a shot of something extra when we weren't looking? Like straight caffeine or something?" I asked. Zack and Lisa just shook their heads, we all laughed.

Chapter 9

Lisa bought us a round of Blowjob shots, which caused me and Hannah to blush like crazy. She snickered at Brock and Zack who failed miserably at taking their shots, "Looks like you two need some more practice."

Brock scoffed, "As if! I think I handled that like a pro." Zack just shook his head and looked down. He had some whipped cream stuck to the tip of his nose, I stroked his nose with my finger and took the cream off. I licked my fingertip and wiggled my eyebrows at him. Zack's eyebrows shot up and he let his jaw fall slightly as he watched me.

"Alright girls, let's show them how it's done! Hands behind your backs!" Lisa announced. I intertwined my fingers behind my back and leaned forward with my mouth wide. I pulled the shot glass into my mouth, swirled my tongue and flipped the drink up to pour the alcohol down my throat in one go. Lisa did the same but Hannah had trouble breaking the seal and ended up coughing like crazy. Brock patted her back softly to try and help.

Lisa laughed, poor Hannah was red faced from both coughing and embarrassment. I looked at Zack, he smiled at me, "You did very well with that one." I winked at him, "Practice." I scolded myself internally for winking, I had no idea what had gotten into me. Zack leaned forward until his lips were an inch from mine, he whispered, "That's hot, Layla." It may have been the shots but I felt bold so I leaned forward and pecked his lips with mine quickly. Zack didn't have time to react to me but as I pulled away he stared at me, his cheeks bright red. I smiled at him and sat back in my chair.

We ended up closing the bar down that night. Sarah never did show up. Brock decided to sleep his drunk off in his truck. Hannah's sister came to pick us up. I shook my head and took Zack's hand in mine, "Would you like to walk me home?" He nodded eagerly. I took his hand and led him away from the crowd. We walked together, holding hands across the parking lot.

I lived about seven blocks from the bar, as it was a small town. Zack and I didn't say anything as we walked. He held my hand tightly, squeezing it from time to time. I smiled to myself, not sure what was going to happen once we got to my place, but I was happy he was with me. We passed by the library where there were some benches. Zack pulled me over to one of them and sat down. He pulled me onto his lap and kissed my cheek softly. His arms moved around my waist and held me tight. I smiled at him, "What are you up to?"

"Look at those stars, Layla. Aren't they beautiful?" he asked. I looked up. The night was very clear, you could see all the stars. I tried to find a few constellations and point them out to him. He told me some of the ones he knew as well. It was after 2am, so it was quiet in the park. I whispered into Zack's ear, "You should kiss me." He leaned his face to mine and pressed our lips together. I kissed him back softly. I let my hand trail up to flow through his dark hair. Zack let out a soft moan at my touch, his own hands moving down my back to rest on my hips.

Before things could get too heated I jumped off his lap and pulled him with me, "Come on, baby, let's keep moving." Zack chuckled and nodded. He followed me as I led him out of the park and across the street toward my house. When we got to my front door I unlocked it and turned to Zack. He smiled drunkenly at me, "Can I come in?" I smirked at him, "Do you think you deserve to?"

Zack scoffed, "I think I've been a very good boy!" I laughed and pulled him into my house, closing the door behind us. I kissed him passionately as we made our way across my living room. Zack pushed me softly up against a wall and let his hands flow from my hips up to the back of my neck. I explored his mouth with my tongue, he tasted like beer and irish cream, it was an oddly intoxicating combination. He eagerly let me and twisted our tongues together. I rested my hands on his biceps, squeezing them slightly.

"You are so sexy, Layla." he whispered into my mouth. I sighed and returned his kisses urgently. I really wanted to do sexual things with him but I knew we were both too drunk for it to be a good idea. My mind was swirling with all kinds of scenarios, but before I could make up my mind Zack slid his hand under my shirt and up to cup my breast. I moaned and nibbled on his lip. He maneuvered my breasts out of my bra and caressed them both with his rough hands. I could tell he was enjoying their size by the moaning coming from his throat. I pulled my shirt off over my head to take the barrier away between us.

Zack stared down at my fully exposed chest and smiled. He began teasing my nipples in between his massage movements of my breasts. I gasped when he pinched particularly hard and cried out, "Oh god, that hurts!" He whispered his apologies into my ear and trailed his lips down to my tender nipples. Zack twirled his tongue around them one at a time before returning to my lips, "There, all better."

I started to unbutton his shirt when Zack stopped me, whispering, "Am I staying over?" I raised my eyes to meet him and nodded, "But we aren't having sex."

He whined against my neck, "How come? I have a condom." I shook my head and pulled his shirt off exposing his chest. I started to kiss his pecs and collarbone, which seemed to drive him crazy. I trailed my tongue from his shoulder up to to his ear to hiss, "I'm not fucking you tonight, but we can do other stuff. Take it or leave it, Zack."

As I bit down hard on his earlobe he cried out, "Ok, ok, I'll take what I can get. What can I have?" I let my hot lips trail down his neck again before I took a step back from him, "Come on, I'll show you." I took his hand and pulled him into my bedroom. Zack followed me eagerly. We got rid of our pants and underwear, at some point our shoes had come off but I wasn't sure when that happened. I pushed him back onto the bed and gestured for him to scoot up to the headboard.

I crawled onto my bed like a panther ready to strike. Zack sucked in a deep breath as I trailed my fingers up his thigh and wrapped them around his member. I began to pump him slowly, in a teasing fashion, "Do you think you have been a good boy?"

"Yes, oh god, yes!" he cried out. I squeezed him tighter, but didn't increase my pace. I whispered into his ear, "Do you think you have been good enough to deserve this?" Zack nodded eagerly, his eyes closed tight as he threw his head back. My fingers tightened around him a bit more and my wrist sped up slightly. I moved the fingertips of my left hand overtop of his tip and stroked in a circular motion. Zack let out a series of curse words as I pumped him faster. When I knew he was close I moved my fingers from his tip to just behind his testicles to massage his prostate. Zack cried out as he came all over his stomach and my hand. I pumped him slowly until he was empty and sighing softly before I stood up to get a towel.

As I wiped my hand off he looked up at me with hazy eyes, "Wow, that was the best old fashioned I have ever had. Amazing, Layla." I nodded and wiped off his stomach for him. I grabbed my nightgown from under my pillow and slipped it on. Zack looked up at me, his eyes concerned, "What are you doing?"

"I'm getting ready for bed. You can sleep on that side or take the couch or walk back to your truck. Whatever you want to do." I told him as I pulled the covers back and slid into bed. He frowned at me, "What do you mean the couch or my truck? Why would I leave?" I shrugged, "I dunno. Whatever you want to do."

He slipped under the covers next to me and shuffled over to me, kissing my face softly, "This is what I want to do." He moved his hands up to my chest again and massaged my breasts. Zack's right hand left my chest and slid down my side to my thigh. He lifted my nightgown up a bit and started to caress my inner thigh gently. I sighed and whimpered slightly. He smiled against my lips, "I want to touch you, too." I nodded, granting him permission.

"Let me hear you, Layla. I want to know if you enjoy it." he told me. I sighed as he slipped his fingers over my clit and core. I bucked my hips as he drew small circles on my bundle of nerves and let out a long, loud moan. As he slid two fingers into me I cried out, he froze, not expecting me to be so tight. Zack moved back slightly and stroked his fingers inside me slowly, he looked down into my eyes, "Are you a virgin, baby?" I could feel my cheeks turn crimson as I nodded. I whispered, "Technically, yes."

He leaned down and kissed me so slowly I thought time had stopped. His lips were so soft and tender I melted into him. Zack moved his hand carefully inside me, taking special care with each movement. He whispered against my lips, "So tight and so beautiful." I smiled and slipped my tongue into his mouth. He lapped at my tongue with his as he flicked his wrist to rub my clit a bit harder. I started to tremble as my orgasm rolled off my body in waves. My core tightened around his fingers, which stilled his movements. I rode out my euphoria with his name on my lips.

As I was coming down from my high Zack stroked his fingers between my walls carefully, "Did I hurt you?" I shook my head and kissed him again. He sighed softly as he continued to stroke me. I chuckled into his mouth, "Are you just going to stay in there?"

He nodded and kissed my forehead, "You feel so amazing. I love being inside you. You feel like warm liquid velvet wrapped around a vice, it's so fucking sexy." I cried out at his embarrassing words. No one had ever described my vagina in such a way before. I buried my face in his shoulder and giggled. Zack kissed the side of my head, around my cheek until he found my lips. I kissed him back as he continued to slide his fingers in and out of me gently.

I felt another orgasm begin to build from his teasing, which caused me to sigh and pull his face closer to mine. I moaned into his mouth, "Zack, don't stop... oh god!" He groaned and continued to stroke me as I tightened my core around his fingers. He whispered into my ear, "Come again for me, Layla. So beautiful, I want you so bad." His words pushed me over the edge and I cried out in pleasure. I wrapped my arms around his neck and held on as I trembled. I'd never had two orgasms back to back with a partner before, and those orgasms were incredible on their own. As I came down Zack kissed my neck over and over again, "You are amazing, baby, just amazing."

At some point we fell asleep. Before I knew it, the sun was sneaking in through the window. I forced my eyes open to see a mess of clothing scattered across my bedroom floor. Zack was sound asleep next to me, taking up more than his share of the bed. I stared at his naked body and the realization of what we had done the night before came back to me. I had let him stay over and we had fooled around. I rubbed my face with my palms roughly, annoyed with myself. I hadn't planned on bringing him home with me, I'd had a moment of weakness. As I stood up and slipped my housecoat over my nightgown I thought back to our time together and how good it felt. I had to admit, Zack had given me some mind blowing orgasms, but I wasn't sure how he would feel about what we did in the light of day.

I left the room and went to my kitchen to make coffee. I sat at the table and waited for the pot to brew in silence. Zack was snoring lightly in my room, completely content. I wasn't sure how to feel about any of it. I ended up standing next to the coffee pot, willing it to brew faster. As I poured myself a cup of coffee I heard my phone ringing in my bedroom. I ran quickly to try and grab it before Zack woke up but I was too late. He rolled over and smiled sleepily at me as I answered my cell, "Hello?"

"Hey, Layla, sorry to call so early but I am going to ask you to come over and help me with some deep cleaning at my mom's house. Can you come by after lunch?" Jackie was talking really fast into her phone. I nodded at first, before realizing she couldn't see me. I told her I'd be over after lunch before quickly hanging up my phone.

Zack stared up at me with a grin on his face, he didn't even try to cover himself up as he moved around naked in my bed. I rolled my eyes and muttered, "I've got to be somewhere this afternoon so you should get up and get moving." He wiggled his eyebrows at me and reached up to grasp my hand, "Or you could come back to bed and we could snuggle up a bit." I let him pull me to his chest and kiss me, though honestly I wasn't sure about it. I didn't kiss him back but I did tangle my fingers in his hair.

"What's wrong, Layla?" he asked when he realized I wasn't returning his kisses. I shrugged, "I don't know. I've never had a guy stay overnight before. They usually leave before morning." Zack sighed and kissed my forehead, "Well, I didn't. I wanted to sleep next to you all night." I rolled my eyes at him and smiled, "You are a dork you know." He laughed and kissed me again, this time I returned it. I let myself sink into his kisses and wrapped my arms around his neck. I could feel his excitement growing along my inner thigh, which Zack didn't even try to hide.

I leaned back slightly and bit my lower lip, "So it doesn't bother you that I am a virgin?" He shook his head, "Absolutely not, I think it's sexy that you are saving yourself for someone worthy. I want it to be me." I blushed and nibbled on his neck, "Down boy, you will have to wait and see." Zack groaned into my neck and searched for my lips. He crashed our mouths together in a sloppy kiss. I pulled away from him after a few minutes, "Come on, Zack, let's get up and have coffee." He reluctantly trailed after me, but not before pulling his boxers on as we left my bedroom.

Chapter 10

I ended up pushing Zack into his truck back at the bar parking lot in order to get him to go home. He offered to come with me to Jackie's house but I refused. He wanted to get together that night but I said no. When I started walking to my car he followed me and wrapped his arms around my torso, "Alright, can I at least have a goodbye kiss, baby?"

I rolled my eyes and attempted to kiss him quickly, but Zack deepened it and held on to me a bit tighter. I pushed him off slightly and whispered, "Just because we hooked up, that doesn't mean we are a couple now. It was just a night of fun." Zack's face fell, he released his embrace around me suddenly. He took a step back and stuffed his hands into his pockets.

"So, after last night, we are still nothing?" he asked. His voice was laced with sadness. He wasn't trying to hide it, his eyes held disappointment. I sighed before I spoke, "Not nothing, just not official. I'm just not interested in that, sorry."

Zack looked down at the ground, he didn't meet my eyes, "So you have other guys in your life?" I shook my head, "Not right now, no. I do date though. I'm not holding you to anything and you shouldn't hold me to anything either."

I crossed my arms over my chest, I knew I sounded harsh but I didn't want to lead him on. Zack was a nice guy but I didn't trust him yet, and I wasn't sure I would ever be able to. I enjoyed what we had done, but one night didn't equal a relationship. I watched him kick the ground under his shoes. Zack sighed and nodded, "So, we are just friends with benefits then? That's all I am?"

I shook my head, "I wouldn't even give it that title. We hooked up once, just once." He swore and turned his back to me, "Wow, that's harsh, Layla. But I guess it's my turn to be pushed into the lockers." Zack walked back to his truck and climbed inside. I thought about running after him but I didn't. Maybe it was true, maybe I just wanted to punish him a little for hurting me years ago, maybe I wasn't ready for anything more. I wasn't sure exactly what I felt, all I knew was I didn't want to rush into anything with Zack and I had to keep him in check.

I watched him pull out of the parking lot, sending gravel flying and a cloud of dust in his wake. I sighed and climbed into my car to go home. I showered and thought about how I'd handled the whole thing with Zack. I wasn't proud of myself, I felt guilty. He obviously wanted more from me than I wanted from him. However I wasn't willing to enter into a relationship just because he wanted me to, I wasn't in a place where I wanted that. I'd never lied to him about what we were, I'd been honest. It would have been more cruel to lead him on and let him think we were more.

Jackie had asked me to pick up some Javex from the Co-Op so I ran to the store on my way to his place. As I was going through the cleaning aisle I ran into Hannah. She smiled when she saw me and pulled her cart up next to mine, "So, how did it go?"

I frowned, "It was fine. He went home this morning." She giggled, "Oh that's awesome! Are you seeing him tonight?" I shook my head.

"Why does everyone think a hook-up equals a relationship? We aren't dating, we aren't anything. It was once, that's it." I told her, annoyed. Hannah's face fell, she took a step back from me, "You just kicked him to the curb?"

I nodded. She sighed loudly, "That's terrible, Layla. Zack really likes you and you just kicked him out. That's harsh." I rolled my eyes, "It was a hook-up, that's it."

Hannah shook her head, "Not to him, and you know that. He likes you, I bet he's sitting at home licking his wounds right now." I chuckled and shrugged, "Well maybe it's his turn to hurt a little bit."

She slapped my arm, "Layla, that's cruel! You knew he was crazy about you and you used him. That's terrible! You are better than that!" I stared into Hannah's face, "Why is it if a guy hooks up it's ok but if a woman does it, she is a cruel, heartless bitch? I never told him I wanted more than a night. Zack is an adult, he can make his own decisions. I never promised him anything. I didn't lead him on."

Hannah shook her head, "I think you do like him and you are scared. I think you are comfortable being alone and afraid to be with someone who could actually love you." I stepped back, "This is not the conversation you have at the grocery store. I'll talk to you later." I walked past her quickly and ducked down the dairy aisle. I couldn't get away from her fast enough as she uttered the word 'love'.

Chapter 11

Jackie was already in one of the spare bedrooms of her mom's house packing up the knick-knacks and fabrics by the time I got there. Her mom was watching T.V. in the living room. I found my way to Jackie and announced my arrival.

"Did you bring the Javex?" she asked. I nodded and showed her the grocery bag. We didn't chat much, she put me straight to work in the basement. I was sent to pack up her mom's sewing room. There were already a bunch of collapsed banker's boxes against the wall. Jackie said her mom couldn't sew anymore, it was too difficult for her hands and her mind so everything had to go. I opened a large floor length closet to find piles and piles of fabric folded neatly. It looked like thousands of dollars worth of material in one space.

The sewing room took me about two hours to completely pack up before I even got to the cleaning part. Jackie came down to check my progress, she brought me a cold beer for my efforts. She looked around the room and smiled, "Great work, Layla. I wish I could just hire you." I chuckled and shook my head.

We sat down on the carpet and drank our beers. Jackie was thrilled she had finally talked her mom into moving in with her, "It will be so much easier. We can sell this house and that will give us a nice cushion for her care." I nodded in agreement.

"So, how was the bar last night? I wish I could have gone." she asked. I shrugged, "It was alright. We drank way too much. Lisa got us Blowjob shots, so that was a hoot." We laughed out loud and sipped our beers.

Jackie looked at me with serious eyes, "So, Hannah texted me this morning..." I rolled my eyes, "Don't start, Jackie. I don't want to hear it." She sighed and nodded. Jackie knew me better than anyone. She knew I didn't want a relationship and she was fully aware of my desire to keep a distance from Zack. She'd been there every single time I cried from the bullying. Jackie knew all about my casual relationships since highschool, that I didn't let guys get too close to me. She never judged me.

"I remember Zack. He was a jerk to you in highschool." she muttered. I nodded, "Yeah he was. He's matured though." Jackie smiled at me, "Well that's good. Do you think he's mature enough to handle a casual hook-up situation?" I shrugged, "He didn't take it very well this morning when I told him we weren't starting something. I'm not sure honestly."

She nodded and took another sip of her beer, "Hey at least you are getting some. I haven't been with anyone in over two years. I'm starting to find the old guy in the meat department sexy. I think he's got to be sixty-five." I laughed along with Jackie. I smiled and suggested, "Well you could try a dating app. You might get lucky." She shook her head, "No, not right now. I'm not in a place where dating is really an option. Maybe some-day."

I left shortly after we finished our beer. My body was sore from the packing and cleaning, I decided I wanted to take a bath when I got home. Mr. Fuzz was sitting in the window waiting for me as I pulled into the driveway. I ate a quick meal of mi-crowave ravioli and filled up my bathtub with scented bubbles. I lit a couple candles and let myself float away. I was almost in a complete state of zen when my phone went off. I chose to ignore it and let the bubbles do the heavy lifting.

Before I went to bed I checked my phone. It was a text from Sarah inviting me out that night to the bar. I didn't bother reply-ing, I had no interest in going out two nights in a row. I crawled into bed and let the softness of my pillow take me away to dreamland, while I tried to ignore the delicious smell of Zack's shampoo on my pillows.

Chapter 12

I was rudely awoken by my phone ringing. I sat up with a start, launching Mr. Fuzz. I hadn't noticed he was sleeping on my shoulder so when I sat up with a start, I accidentally sent my cat flying to the foot of the bed. Through hooded eyes I glared at my clock next to my bed, it was 2:44am. What the actual fuck, why was my phone ringing. Then my eyes shot open, realizing it was probably bad news.

I reached over and answered my cell, not even looking at who was calling, "Hello!"

"Hey, baby, I need a ride. I'm way too drunk to drive home tonight." a loud, slurring voice shouted into my ear. I yawned into my phone and closed my eyes, as I flopped back down on my bed.

"Who is this?" I groaned. I heard a laugh come down the phone, "It's the guy you kicked out this morning. Can you please come get me?" It was Zack, and he was wasted. I sighed, "Zack, just sleep in your truck."

Zack let a hic-up go through the line as he slurred, "I got a ride with Brock and he took some girl home with him tonight.

Everyone else has left, the bar is locked up and I have nowhere to go. I wouldn't bother you if I had anyone else to call."

"Fucking hell, Zack. Fine. I'll be right there." I muttered and hung up the phone. I didn't bother getting dressed, I just threw my jacket on, grabbed my keys and ran out the door. I drove to the bar and found Zack sitting out front on the curb. He winced his eyes as I blared my headlights into his face.

Zack got up with great difficulty from the curb and wobbled his way over to the passenger side of my car. I unlocked it for him as he tugged on the door handle. He opened the door and dropped onto the seat inside. I glared at him but all Zack did was smile wide at me. He blew me a kiss and smirked, "Hey baby, you are the best."

"Uh-huh." I muttered, "Put your seatbelt on, Zack." He did as I instructed. I didn't look at him, I just put my car into reverse and asked, "Do you want me to take you to your mom's house?"

He shook his head, "No, she will lose her shit if I show up looking like this. Can I stay at your place?" I groaned, "Zack, I was asleep! I hate this!"

Zack leaned over to my side of the car and kissed my cheek, "Please, baby, I have nowhere to go. I'll sleep on the floor if you want, just let me stay at your house." I rolled my eyes but nodded. I took him to my place. He smiled at me as I pulled into the driveway.

I dragged him into the house and took my jacket off. Zack fell face first onto the floor. He had been trying to take off his shoes but in his drunk state he fell down. He started laughing loudly and shaking his head. I sighed and leaned down to help him with his shoes. Once they were off, I took his jacket off and pulled it off his shoulders.

Zack smiled up at me from the floor, "You are so nice, Layla. So nice to me, nice to everyone. No one would believe you kicked me out this morning." I sighed and shook my head, "Zack…"

He waved me off, "No, I get it. You don't want anything serious. I get it. I just thought maybe what we did last night was special. But it's all good, I know it's not special to you."

"Come on, drunky, you can sleep in my bed. No funny business though. I was sound asleep when you called so don't even try." I warned him. Zack nodded as I pulled him up to a standing position. I took his hand in mine and guided him to my room. Zack slipped out of his jeans and fell face first onto my bed. He was sound asleep in minutes. I covered him with my blanket and shuffled him over slightly so he wasn't on my side.

As I crawled into bed next to him I stared into his face. Zack was a very annoying man but I found myself smiling at him.

He'd woken me up in the dead of night, yet I still felt compelled to go and pick him up in his drunken state. I wasn't angry with him, I hadn't made him walk home to his mother's. Instead, I'd allowed him to stay with me, not only in my house but in my bed. As I adjusted my body to get more comfortable, Zack rolled completely over to face me. His eyes fluttered open, before focusing on me.

He smiled at me and shuffled closer, "Your bed is so comfy, Layla. I love how soft it is." I nodded, "I'm glad it's up to your expectations." Zack chuckled, "You are awesome."

I sighed, "Go to sleep, Zack. I'm tired, just let me sleep." He leaned forward and kissed my forehead, "Ok, good night baby." I frowned and rolled onto my back away from him, "Knock off the 'baby' shit."

Zack closed his eyes and hummed slightly, as though he didn't really hear me. In a few moments I heard him snoring softly again. I closed my own eyes and let myself drift off to sleep.

When I woke up in the morning, Mr. Fuzz was resting on my chest, purring lightly. I glanced down to see behind him was an arm that wasn't mine. Zack had wrapped his arm around my waist and was snuggled up with his face in the crook of my neck, sound asleep. He wasn't snoring, he was just breathing softly. I closed my eyes again and let myself breathe him in, he smelled so delicious.

Mr. Fuzz and lay awake together for a while, snuggled up with Zack. I wanted to wake him up, but he looked so peaceful next to me I didn't have the heart to. I listened to his breathing, I could feel his steady heartbeat through my side. It felt oddly comfortable to wake up with him, I wasn't expecting to feel that way.

Zack started to stir about thirty minutes after I woke up. He nuzzled further into my neck and moaned softly, "Layla? Mmmm, you smell good." I chuckled, "That's good to hear. How are you feeling?"

"My head hurts, I feel like I was hit by a truck." he muttered into my neck. I sighed, "I've got Tylenol and Advil if you want, it's in the cabinet in the bathroom." I felt Zack smile, which sent a shiver down my neck.

I cleared my throat as I told him, "I can make you some breakfast if you want. I've got eggs, bacon and toast. I mean, only if you want." Zack pulled me closer to his chest and sighed, "You are taking such good care of me, Layla." I chuckled and shrugged. We laid there together for a few minutes before I moved to get up. Zack groaned but allowed me to move

I pulled on my housecoat and shuffled to the doorway of my bedroom. I glanced back at Zack watching me, his eyes were tired but they seemed happy. Mr. Fuzz sat at the foot of the bed, also watching me. I whispered, "Take a shower, Zack. I'll make us some breakfast."

Chapter 13

I cracked the eggs into the pan and flipped them over-easy. I had no idea how Zack liked his eggs but I liked mine over-easy so I just made him the same thing. The bacon was crispy, I nibbled on a piece as I finished off our breakfasts. Zack shuffled out of my bathroom towel drying his hair. He was only in his boxer shorts which made me chuckle, "Come on and eat before it gets cold. Do you want coffee?"

He nodded and came up next to me at the table. I ushered him to a seat and put two eggs on the plate in front of him. Zack smiled up at me, "Wow, this is awesome. Thanks Layla." I smiled softly at him as I took two mugs from the cupboard and filled them with coffee. I set one down in front of Zack while I crossed the table to take my seat. We ate in quiet contemplation, stealing glances at each other now and then. Mr. Fuzz demanded bacon from us, which was hilarious.

When we finished our breakfast Zack's eyes met mine, "What are you doing today?" I glanced at the clock; it read 9:33am. I sighed, "Well, I should probably get some groceries today for the week. Then I will do some laundry and clean the litter box. Mr. Fuzz will not be happy with me if I don't clean it out."

He chuckled as he wiped his plate with the last bits of toast. I always found it interesting when men did that, as a way to clean the plate before washing it. My father had done that as well, the simple gesture tugged at my heartstring a little. As I sipped my coffee I asked, "So how come you got so tanked last night?"

Zack looked down at the table, avoiding my eyes. He cleared his throat awkwardly and ran his hands through his hair, "I don't know. I hadn't planned on it. I just started drinking with Brock, he kept buying shots and… I don't know… I guess I just lost track of how much I had." I nodded and finished my cup of coffee. As I stood up to get another cup I mumbled, "You know, if you drank too much because you were sad about yesterday morning we can talk about it."

He sighed, "What's there to talk about? You kicked me out, you don't want anything more. It's fine." I shook my head, "If it was fine, you wouldn't have mentioned it so many times last night when you were drunk."

"You don't owe me an explanation, Layla. I know you don't want anything serious from me." he told me. Zack's voice came out unsteady, almost shy. I cleared my throat as I filled up my mug, "I didn't want to hurt you. It's not personal, you know. I just don't date seriously, I never really have. Relationships make me uneasy."

Zack looked up to meet my eyes as I sat down across from him, "Have you ever been in a relationship?" I shook my head, blushing slightly. I was twenty-six and I'd never been in a serious relationship. He smiled at me, "I haven't really either. The longest I've dated anyone was a year and that was not a very good experience. It was only really good for the first six months."

I chuckled, "I know it seems weird that I haven't had any serious relationships but it's not because I haven't been asked. It's more because I just didn't have time for someone in a serious way." He rolled his eyes, "I get it. I really do. We can be friends, Layla."

As I tucked my hair behind my ears and felt a small tingle in my stomach, "I do like spending time with you, Zack." His eyes shot to mine, a smile crept across his lips, "I like you, Layla."

"Maybe we could hang out sometimes. No labels, no rules, no commitments. Nothing serious, but just two adults having some fun." I suggested. Zack sat back in his chair and smirked, "I'm suddenly very aware that I am in my underwear right now."

I looked away and laughed. He crossed his arms over his chest and grinned at me, "So you want to have a friends with benefits thing? Is that what you are suggesting?" I met Zack's eyes with a smirk, "We could if you are interested. We could work something out."

Zack stood up to refill his mug. He added sugar and stirred his coffee. He leaned back against my countertop and sipped his coffee, "Do you have arrangements with anyone else?" I shook my head. He smiled, "Ok. If we are doing this we need some ground rules."

"Well, for starters we don't advertise it. We keep things quiet between us." I told him. Zack frowned for a moment, "So we deny that we spend time together?"

I shook my head, "No, we can hang out in public together, we just don't advertise that we are together." He shrugged, "Alright. That's fine. I want to spend time with you regularly, two or three nights a week." I nodded, "That's reasonable."

"No labels. That's not optional." I said sternly. Zack chuckled and rolled his eyes, "Yes you have been very clear about that. No labels. However, I want to be exclusive. Just the two of us." I shook my head, "No, Zack, I'm not willing to offer that. Sorry."

He groaned and rubbed the back of his neck, annoyed, "Fine, but if either of us is seeing someone else we have to talk about it. Deal?" I smiled softly and nodded.

I stood up and crossed the kitchen to stand in front of him, I pulled his hands from behind his neck and wrapped them around my waist. Zack smiled at me as I wrapped my arms around his shoulders. He asked with a cocky grin, "What about sex?"

I bit my lower lip and whispered, "I'm technically a virgin, but I'm not opposed to changing that if the time is right. However, I would prefer to start out slow and work our way there." He nodded, "I agree. I don't want to rush anything either."

Zack leaned forward and kissed my lips softly, he squeezed my hips slightly. I returned his kiss and ran my hand through his soft dark hair. I savored his flavor as we explored each other's mouths. I moaned slightly which seemed to spear him on. He pulled away for a moment to whisper in my ear, "God you are so sexy, Layla." I pulled his face back into another kiss.

When we finally broke apart we were both panting. I smiled at Zack, "You are a really good kisser, you know." He nodded and smiled, "One more request, I want to call you baby." I scrunched up my nose at him, which caused Zack to chuckle, "Come on, Layla. It's a cute endearment. Just give me that."

"Fine. You can call me baby. I'll try to come up with something to call you." I teased. He nodded, "Good, you can call me pretty much anything, baby." I kissed his cheek and nodded. I wasn't sure what we had just started, but it felt like something interesting.

Chapter 14

Days turned into weeks and the weather started to cool off with the dawn of fall. Jackie had sold her mom's house and we were in the process of moving her into Jackie's place. Her mom wasn't much help with everything, she was usually in a bad mood about the whole thing. Jackie was exhausted and she was having a hard time with all the responsibilities. I did my best to help her out but a lot of the things that needed to be done I was unable to help with.

She sent me a text message one afternoon while I was on my coffee break at work. Jackie wanted to know if I knew anyone with a truck to help her move some larger furniture from one house to the other. Zack was sitting across from me, fiddling on his own phone. I glanced up at him and smirked, "Hey, do you think you could help my friend Jackie out this weekend with moving some furniture with your truck?"

He glanced up at me, "Of course." He made me smile, Zack was so simple and easy. He didn't make it complicated, he was just happy to lend a hand. I smiled and texted Jackie back that we could help out on Saturday. She was thrilled and thanked me profusely. I chuckled, "Jackie says 'thank you, thank you, thank you'."

Zack smiled and nodded, "Anytime baby. You are coming with me right? I mean, I know Jackie but not very well." I nodded, reassuring him that he wouldn't' have to help out my friend without me. Brock came over to join our table and sat down next to Zack with a thump, "Jackie? That girl who works at the Co-Op? She's hot!"

I rolled my eyes, "Yes Brock, my friend Jackie is moving her mother into her house this weekend." His eyes lit up, "You know her? I want to meet her! Can I come?"

I frowned at him, "Brock, you know her already. We all graduated together. You went to school with her for two years." His face fell, he looked confused, "No we didn't. I'd remember a hottie like her." I sighed, "She and I were always together. Do you remember a tall girl with braces and glasses? She had pretty bad acne back then, it didn't clear up until she was about twenty."

Brock's mouth dropped open, "Chicken neck? That's the girl who works at the Co-Op? No way!" I pursed my lips, "God you are an asshole. You don't even know her name, you just pick some stupid nick-name. Yes, that is my friend Jackie."

Zack chuckled, "Smooth, man. Good job." Brock smacked his shoulder and stared at me, "Layla, you have to help me out. I've been trying to meet her for ages. I would love to get to know her, is she single?"

I shook my head, "No way, Brock! You are the LAST guy I would introduce to my dearest friend. Besides, don't you have a few different girls on the line? Just go with one of them!" Zack laughed out loud at my statement. Brock sighed, "Girls from the bar don't count as relationships."

My stomach turned at the idea of Jackie and Brock together. He was such a player and she was way too kind and trusting to handle someone like him. Brock would use her and throw her away before Jackie even knew what had happened. There was no way in hell I was going to let that get too far. I glared at him, "What about you and Hannah? What happened to that?"

Brock's face fell and he stared down at the table between us, "She told me I wasn't what she was looking for, alright. It was embarrassing enough to be blown off by a girl in the first place." I cocked my head to the side and tried not to smirk, somehow knowing Hannah had shut him down filled me with petty satisfaction. I pushed it to the side and said, "Well, that doesn't mean all of my friends are up for grabs. You want to meet her, go and introduce yourself to her at the Co-Op. I can guarantee she remembers you, and you won't get very far."

Brock grunted, "That's not fair! High school was a long time ago! I'm different now." I rolled my eyes and shot back, "Really? Did you try to steal my lunch like a month ago? We are twenty-six now, what's your excuse for that?"

"That was a joke, jeez Layla. Come on." Zack shook his head, "No man, you reap what you sow. You and I both know that now." I smiled at him, he returned my smile with a soft wink. Brock rolled his eyes, "Oh shut up, Zack. You aren't helping."

Brock sighed before he stood up, "I've got a truck and I'll help out all day. Just think about it, Layla. I'd love to meet her, please think about it." He turned his back to us and left the break room to head back to work. My eyes followed him until he was out of earshot, "Yeah, Zack, he's not coming to help Jackie. No way. Not going to happen."

He chuckled and rolled his eyes, "Alright, alright. I won't let him come. Relax." I frowned at him, "I'm serious, the last thing she needs is Brock Hansen coming in a fucking up her life. He would just cut and run, I'm not going to let him do that to her."

Zack smiled at me with kind eyes, "Layla, baby, she's a big girl. Trust me, Brock has already screwed up with her anyway, I mean, he doesn't even remember her from school. You've got nothing to worry about." I raised my eyebrows at him in a warning gesture. "I better not."

"Alright, I'll take care of it. Brock won't bother her. Relax baby." he whispered, his hands up in surrender. I nodded, "Alright, thank you." Zack and I stood up together and walked toward the break room door. He leaned over to whisper in my ear, "Want to have dinner tonight and a sleepover? I can cook."

I smirked at him, "Sure. Don't forget to bring your pajamas." He blushed slightly before nodding and turning to head back to his station. I watched Zack walk down the hallway, his hands in his pockets. He was such a cutie, I thought to myself. He turned back and caught me checking him out, he smirked and winked at me. I felt my face burn with embarrassment. I quickly turned around and rushed back to my station. When I got there, I found my supervisor waiting for me.

Chapter 15

"Layla, hey, I was wondering if you could stay after work today for some overtime? We are running a bit behind today." Trevor informed me. I smiled at him, "Sure I can do that. I have dinner plans though so I can't stay past 6pm."

Trevor nodded, "No worries, it will probably only be an hour or so. Thanks, Layla. You are always a team player." I blushed and nodded as I returned to my work. I had always liked Trevor, he was such a nice man. My crush on him had dissipated since I'd been spending time with Zack but I had to admit as he walked away, I checked him out.

I met with Zack after work to lend him my house keys. He frowned when I told him I'd accepted overtime, "But we have a date!" I rolled my eyes, "Yes and I'll be there for it. You can let yourself into my house and start making supper. You wanted to cook for me right? Wasn't that your whole plan?"

Zack took my keys and looked at me annoyed, "Yeah, but I thought we were going to hang out together while I did." I offered him a sweet smile, "I'll only be an hour or so. You might not even be at my place by the time I get off work. I'll see you soon, ok?" He nodded. I felt Zack watching me as I went back to work. I giggled to myself, what a silly man I thought.

The overtime ended up only being about forty-five minutes. I clocked out and headed out of the locker room when I met

Trevor. He smiled at me, "Thanks for your help today again." I nodded and returned his smile, "Of course. Anytime." He held the exit door open for me, which I thought was very thoughtful.

Trevor walked with me to my car. He and I exchanged pleasantries and discussed the weather mostly. When we reached my car Trevor stood next to me, leaning against the hood. He was handsome, I examined his strong features and plump lips, he was making me think naughty thoughts. I ran my hand through my hair nervously, I realized Trevor was smiling at me. My breath caught in my chest for a moment before I said, "Well you probably should head home to your family. I'm sure they are waiting for you."

Trevor sighed heavily, "Actually, my wife and I separated about a month ago. We've had some problems for the last couple of years. So I'm living with my brother and his wife for now." My face fell, "Oh, I'm sorry to hear that."

He shook his head, not making eye contact with me, "It's ok. It was a while coming. We are just very different people. I still see my baby girl all the time, that's what's most important right now." I nodded, "Of course, yeah. It's still rough though."

"It is. I'd appreciate it if you didn't mention it to anyone at work. I don't exactly want the whole factory knowing about my personal life." he muttered. I smiled, "Oh yeah, I get it. Trust me, relationship stuff is hard to hide in this place. Your secret is safe with me."

Trevor smiled, "Thanks Layla." He reached over and touched my arm softly. I hadn't expected it, but I didn't pull away. He studied my reaction for a moment before he pulled his hand away and shoved his hands into his pockets, "Anyway, I'll see you tomorrow."

I nodded and moved away to the driver's side of my car. Trevor walked past me to his own vehicle, glancing back at me as he did. I turned my head to hide my blushing face. I didn't want my supervisor to see the effect he had on me. I picked up my phone to let Zack know I was on my way home. He responded with a thumbs up.

By the time I returned home I found Zack had made a caesar salad, grilled chicken and mashed potatoes. It was a delicious looking meal, he even had my apron on when I came through the door. Zack had put out white wine and candles for the occasion. I smiled at him as I hung up my jacket, "Wow, you went all out didn't you?"

"You deserve it, baby. You take care of everyone else, so I wanted to make you a nice dinner." he told me as he poured wine into a glass for me. Mr. Fuzz rubbed himself on my legs and meows softly. Zack chuckled, "Don't let him fool you, I fed him right before you got home. He's just playing on your emotions."

I laughed out loud and picked up my cat, "Oh, are you manipulating momma?" Mr. Fuzz purred into my ear. I gave him a tight squeeze before releasing him and crossing the room to Zack. He pecked my lips softly and handed me my glass of wine.

As I took a sip, Zack asked, "So how was the overtime?" I shrugged, "It was alright. I had a visit with Trevor after work for a bit." I sat down at my plate and started to eat. Zack tensed up as he joined me. I didn't meet his eyes as he asked, "Oh? What did he want?"

"Just to talk really. Nothing specific." I knew I was fibbing but Trevor's life wasn't Zack's business. He had asked me specifically not to share his personal information with people who worked at the factory, and since Zack worked there I couldn't tell him anyway.

As we ate, Zack continued to ask about Trevor, "So you two are friends?" I shrugged, "As much as I'm friends with anyone I work with." That didn't seem to ease him at all, instead he sat back in his chair and crossed his arms, "I work with you! Are you friends with him like we are friends?"

My eyes shot up and I glared at Zack, "You don't own me Mister. I can be friends with whoever I want so you better tread carefully. We agreed that if either of us started dating anyone else we would talk about it. I believe that was your condition, and I agreed to it. I have absolutely no reason to hide things from you, Zack."

He sighed heavily and lowered his head, "Sorry, it just bothers me that he might be interested in you. I know we agreed to the conditions, sorry Layla." I shook my head, "There is nothing going on with me and Trevor. Though I won't lie to you, I am attracted to him and I always have been."

Zack's face went white, his eyes shot up to meet mine. I don't think he expected me to be so blunt, but I wasn't going to lie to him about that. He deserved to know how I felt about Trevor, especially if we were involved with each other. He slammed his fork into his mashed potatoes and shoved a pile of them into his mouth. He ate his meal like an angry toddler, scraping his cutlery over the plate.

As we finished our meal I sighed and took my plate to the sink, "You are acting like a child, Zack. Would you rather I lied to you about how I feel? Tell you that I don't like Trevor and keep you in the dark? We agreed to talk about things so I am talking and you are acting like I've cheated on you."

He remained silent, sitting at the table with his back to me. I shook my head, "If you aren't mature enough to handle this kind of relationship, then you need to figure it out soon. I'm not going to lie to you and hide things from you, that's not what we have going on here." Zack flinched slightly and stood up. He turned to me and shoved his hands into his pockets, "No, I can handle it, I'm just jealous ok. You can't expect me not to feel jealous, I'm human. I'm not perfect and I'm not going to pretend for you either. You know that I wanted to be exclusive with you so you can't be surprised that it would sting a little when you tell me you like someone else."

I frowned but nodded, it was true. He had been honest with his feelings so if I expected him to accept me as I was I needed to respect his feelings as well. It wasn't fair to him. I pulled Zack into my arms, "You are right. Sorry. I just don't want to lie to you. I care about you, and you deserve the truth."

He smiled down at me and rested his hands on my hips, "I care about you too, Layla." Slowly, Zack leaned forward and kissed me. It started off light but his touch became more demanding. His lips pressed into mine with passion. I let my hands tangle in his dark hair while his hands trailed back to squeeze my butt. I moaned into his mouth as we pulled each other closer and closer. The energy flowing between us was intensely intoxicating as we moved as one to my bedroom.

Chapter 16

We shuffled to my bedroom, our lips never parting. I pulled Zack's t-shirt over his head and slipped my hands down to the zipper of his jeans. He moaned and buried his face into the crock of my neck. I pushed his jeans and boxers down to his knees, before returning to his chest. I kissed his pecs and stroked his biceps with my fingertips. Zack let gasps escape his lips as he stepped back to step out of his garments. He reached out and cupped my face, smashing his lips back on top of mine with haste. I whimpered slightly from the force, but I wrapped my arms around his torso to pull him closer.

"Mmm Layla." he whispered against my lips. I slid my hand from his arms to chest, past his navel to his member. He felt thick and hard in my hand. I stroked him gently, more to tease than anything. Zack hissed into my mouth and bit my lower lip from the friction. I returned his nibble, which sent a chill through his body, causing him to respond with a shiver.

I released him and stepped back, quickly shedding my own clothes, "Lay down on the bed and get comfortable. I'll be back in a second." Zack smirked at me and jumped onto my bed, landing with a slight bounce. I went into my closet and took out my toy chest. Like most healthy adult women, I had a decent sex toy collection. Though I didn't have many items meant for those with penises, I had a nice fleshlight. It was clear with openings at both ends to make cleaning easy. I looked back at Zack and smirked mischievously, I pulled it out along with a bottle of lubricant.

Zack stared at me as I slowly closed my closet and crossed the room to the end of my bed. His eyes fell to the toy in my hand, he pointed to it, "What is that?"

I held it out and smiled, "It's a sex toy, designed for men. I think you might like it. Would you like to try it?" His eyes grew wide in amazement, "Why do you have sex toys?"

I chuckled and shook my head, "Most women have some sort of sex toy. I just happen to have a variety. I bought this one for my male partners. It's very easy to clean and sterilize so it's safe for you to use, I promise." I climbed onto the bed and sat, cross legged. I held it out for him to examine, Zack took it in his hands.

He swallowed slowly before he spoke, "Will it hurt?" I shook my head, "Not at all, it's meant to simulate a vagina. Put your fingers in there to see how it feels." Zack looked down the cylinder and pushed his index finger inside and moved it around. His eyes widened in amazement.

"It's very tight, are you sure it will fit me?" he asked. I nodded, "We put lubricant inside there and it will stretch to accommodate your size, I am very sure you will fit. Then I move it up and down on your shaft until you come." He bit his lower lip and purred slightly. I could tell Zack was a bit nervous to try it, but this kind of toy was considered very vanilla. I knew tons of single guys who had them in different styles and sizes. Zack played with it carefully, he glanced up and blushed slightly when his eyes met mine, "Ok. We can try it." I smirked and took the fleshlight back from him. I took some lubricant in my fingers and put it inside the cylinder. I also traced Zack's member with the remaining gel on my hand, giving him a few gentle strokes. I positioned myself between his legs and leaned closer to his face to kiss him softly.

"Just relax, this is going to feel really good. I promise." I whispered against his lips. Zack whimpered slightly as I pulled away and ran my hand over his shaft. I lowered the fleshlights over him and pushed it down slowly, he let out a long hiss. I smirked as I started to move the toy over him; up and down.

Zack lay back and closed his eyes, he started to moan almost instantly, "Oh god, that feels so real!" I sighed and tightened my grip slightly, still moving at a slow pace. He raised his hips after a few minutes to meet my hand movements, his breathing became heavier. I moved my hand faster over his shaft, Zack let out a long groan. I continued to stroke him until I noticed his stomach clench, I could tell he was close. I took the fleshlight in both my hands and moved up and down faster and harder, I felt Zack's body shudder under my hands as he erupted into the toy. He let out a few curse words as he came down from ecstasy.

As I slowly removed the toy from his overly sensitive shaft, Zack moaned from the aftershocks of contact between us. I set the fleshlight down at the foot of my bed and climbed up Zack's body. He wrapped his arms around me and flipped us over with me underneath him, his lips on mine in a soft, sweet kiss. I returned it and let my fingers get tangled in his hair.

"Layla, that was incredible. I can't believe it, that thing felt so real. I loved it." he whispered into my ear as he trailed kisses down my neck and over my collarbone. I giggled, "Stick with me, sweetie, I've got lots of tricks."

He chuckled against my skin, sending shivers up my spine, "How can a virgin be so seductive? You are amazing, baby. Sex with you is the best I've ever had and we haven't even done it yet." I smirked and pulled his face up to mine, "We will get there. For now just kiss me and make me feel good." Zack nodded against my lips and moved his fingers down to my clit. He didn't break our kiss as his fingers touched all the right spots to quickly send me tumbling over my own edge. We fell asleep in each other's arms shortly after, basking in our passion's afterglow.

Chapter 17

The rest of the week passed without incident. Trevor didn't offer me any more overtime that week so I was able to spend my evenings with Zack, Lisa and Hannah. On Friday night Lisa suggested we have a BBQ at her place which Zack jumped on, since it would probably be our last chance before the weather got too cold. I said I would make a potato salad and Hannah was going to make a no-bake cheesecake.

"I can grill a great steak." Zack boasted to our table. Lisa chuckled and punched his arm playfully, "Ok, fine but if you burn mine you are not allowed near my grill again." He nodded with a smirk, "Deal!"

Brock approached our table slowly with his hands in his pockets. He looked like a terrified little kid walking up to the popular kid's table. I watched him carefully as we waited for him to speak. The rest of the table acted as though he were invisible.

He cleared his throat, "Hey guys, I think I get it now. I owe you all an apology." Zack cleared his throat, "What's up, Brock?" He swayed slightly, his feet rocking his frame side to side, "I used to be a jerk, and I thought it didn't matter because I was always the leader. I thought it was funny. But it wasn't, and I feel it now. I've been sitting over there by myself, watching you all have a good time and it sucks to not be included."

Hannah smiled, "Yeah, it does." Brock's eyes rose to meet hers, "I'm not perfect but I didn't have to be an asshole. I'm sorry, and I want to start over again if I can. I get it now, so can we just move forward?"

Everyone at the table stared at me, even Brock. Though he had been speaking to all of us, I knew everyone would follow my lead. His bullying had been directed at me for the most part. I knew the rest would wait to see what I had to say first. I nodded slowly and met Brock's eyes, "How about you bring a caesar salad tonight to Lisa's for the BBQ? That would be great."

His face lit up with a huge smile. Before I knew it Brock moved behind me and wrapped his arms around my shoulders tightly, he whispered into my ear, "Thank you Layla. Thank you so much." I froze from his contact, my arms raised slightly in mild shock. Zack's gaze met my eyes, he smiled softly at me. I simply nodded and waited for Brock to let go.

"Alright, sounds good. I've got some beer in my fridge but if you want something stronger bring your own. No one touches my liquor cabinet!" Lisa warned us. Brock finally let me go and sat down next to Zack at the table.

Hannah shook her head, "Lisa, no one wants your terrible spirits. Most of them are just different kinds of tequila." Lisa glared playfully at her, "That's my favorite, and I don't like to share!" Hannah rolled her eyes and smirked.

After work as I was walking out of the locker room I noticed Jackie had texted me. She wanted to know if I wanted to go out for supper. Her aunt was in town from Winnipeg to help with the move the next day. I smiled and responded that we were all going to Lisa's for a BBQ, that she should come and bring her fabulous green bean casserole.

As I approached my car I felt a hand on my shoulder. I spun around to feel Zack's lips on top of mine in a chaste kiss. I let myself melt into him, wrapping my arms around his neck. He whispered against my lips, "You are such a good person, baby. I adore you." I smirked as I broke the kiss, "Yeah, sure. Let's go with that." Zack leaned forward and kissed my forehead softly as we stood next to my car.

"I'll see you at Lisa's. I've been tasked with the grill and I won't disappoint." He reminded me. I laughed out loud, "Yes I agree. If you let Lisa down she will never let any of us forget it. We will be telling that story for decades."

Zack nodded and pecked my lips one more time before he let me go. As he turned to head over to his truck I caught his hand in mine. He looked back at me with a curious smirk. I pulled Zack into my arms and kissed him hard, with as much passion as I could muster. It slipped my mind that we were standing in the parking lot of the factory. I didn't care that our coworkers were walking past us, watching our public display. I just wanted to kiss him one more time, to remind him that I liked him. Zack melted into my embrace and slipped his hand into the back pocket of my jeans, He gave my butt a slight squeeze. When we broke apart, both needing air, he whispered to me, "What was that for, baby?"

I shrugged, "I just felt like it. I don't know, you are making me bolder I guess." Zack kissed my ear softly, his breath tickled, "I like bold Layla. I also like shy Layla and sexy Layla. I like you anyway I can get you, baby. I am crazy about the whole package."

I nodded into his shoulder and let my arms pull back. As we finally separated I watched him walk to his truck. Zack turned back a couple of times and winked playfully at me. I knew I was going to see him in a few short hours, but I still felt a pang of sadness watching him walk away. What a silly sentimental moment I thought to myself.

Chapter 18

Jackie and I decided to go to Lisa's together. I picked her up at 6:15pm. She was thrilled to be going out with friends. As she climbed into my car with her casserole she said, "I can't remember the last time I saw Lisa and Hannah. It's been so long."

I nodded as I pulled away from the curb, "Zack Trulley and Brock Hansen will be there as well. I'm not sure if anyone texted Sarah or not."

Her face formed a frown instantly at the mention of the men's names, "Why are they coming? Since when is Brock Hansen invited anywhere with us?" I sighed heavily, "He works with all of us at the factory and he's Zack's best friend."

She rolled her eyes, "I remember he used to call me 'chicken neck'. One time I was walking down the hallway with a diagram for my science class and he smacked it from underneath as he passed by. It fell out of my hands and broke; I had to ask for an extension to fix it!" I didn't see Jackie's eyes as she recalled the painful memory.

"Yeah I know, he had a couple nicknames for me as well. He's better than he used to be, Brock wants to repair the damage he's done." I told her. She shrugged, seeming unconvinced. I sighed slightly, happy that Jackie wouldn't be easily chased.

She glanced at me, "So what's up with you and Zack? I hear you two are together." I shrugged, "We are spending time together. He's a good guy, he likes me a lot."

"And do you like him?" Jackie asked. I didn't reply, instead I nodded, "I think he's pretty great. But we aren't rushing into any labels right now. We are just seeing where it goes."

As we pulled up to the house, Jackie said to me, "Layla, I've known you for a long time. I know you like to put a distance between yourself and love. Maybe it's time to rethink that?" I scowled at her, "Not yet." I opened my car door and climbed out, retrieving my potato salad from the backseat. She rolled her eyes at me as we walked toward Lisa's front door, "You can't fool me, I know you too well."

I clamped my hand over Jackie's mouth, "SShhh!" She just laughed out loud at me and slapped my hand away. We let ourselves into her house. Hannah was already there. The two of them were in the kitchen drinking beer.

"Jackie! Oh my God, girl, it's so great to see you!" Lisa shouted a little too loudly as she zipped across the room to wrap Jackie up in an embrace. Hannah chuckled and took the casserole so Jackie could return Lisa's hug. I followed Hannah into the kitchen where she offered me a beer.

"The guys aren't here yet?" I asked, trying to keep my voice casual. Hannah smirked at me, "Not yet." I shot her a small glare which only caused her to chuckle at me.

I sent Zack a text to let him know we were at Lisa's. He responded immediately, letting me know he was just getting into his truck. He arrived a few minutes later with Brock in tow. When he saw me, he crossed the kitchen and wrapped his arms around my shoulder, "Sorry I'm late baby, Brock had to change his shirt like three times."

Brock huffed as he followed Zack into the kitchen, "It wasn't three times!" I rolled my eyes. We heard laughter coming from upstairs, Hannah smiled, "I guess Lisa is showing Jackie the new colour she painted the bedroom."

I saw all the colour flow out of Brock's face as he swallowed hard, "Jackie is here? Really? Do I look ok?" He started to fuss with the front of his shirt, smoothing out invisible wrinkles and running his fingers nervously through his hair.

Hannah smiled at him, "Don't worry, Brock, you look fine." Her words didn't seem to soothe him though. As Lisa entered the kitchen, Jackie followed close behind. Brock's eyes rose to meet hers. Jackie's face immediately fell when she saw his face.

"Jackie right? It's nice to see you." Brock managed to choke out. He smiled wide at her, trying desperately hard to make a good impression. She crossed her arms over her chest as she spoke, "Hello Brock Hansen. I'm surprised you know my name." His face fell when she used his full name.

I nudged Zack, "Come on, let's get those steaks going." He kissed the top of my head, "Sounds good, baby. Will you help me?" I smiled at him and nodded. Lisa moved to the fridge and took out the steaks, "Alright, Zack you better not mess these up. Medium rare, nothing else will do!"

Zack let me go and took the large platter from Lisa's hands, "Yes mam. I will not let you down." Hannah chuckled, "Don't be so mean to the man, Lisa. You are just possessive of your grill." Lisa glared at our friend before turning back to Zack, "This is a test to see if you are actually good enough for our Layla. If you fail, then you will never be good enough for her."

"Excuse me, I believe that is my decision, not yours." I told her. Lisa shook her head, "Nope, it's ours. We need to make sure this guy is good enough for our best friend." Zack smirked, "It's ok baby, I don't mind working for your friend's blessing."

I rolled my eyes but couldn't stop a gentle smile from crossing my lips. I followed Zack outside to the grill. He set the steaks down on the table and fired it up. He whispered to me, "I think I may just win your friends over tonight."

"Good for you. Now you just have to win me over." I teased. He turned to me and pulled my hip so my body was flush with his, "Trust me, Layla, I'm working on it." Zack's face was so close to mine, his warm breath fanned my face. I stared into his eyes, I could tell he wanted to say more but before he could I brushed my lips against his.

Zack's hand came up to cup the side of my face. He deepened our kiss slowly while our lips moved in sync with each other. I ran my tongue along the seam of his mouth, requesting entrance. Zack opened his mouth for me to explore. As my hands tangled in his hair I realized I was slowly losing my resolve to keep things casual with this guy, he was breaking down my defences one passionate kiss at a time.

I pulled away slowly, pecking his lips one last time before I whispered, "You are closer than you think." Zack's eyes twinkled slightly as he whispered back, "I know, baby."

Chapter 19

The steaks were medium rare just as Lisa ordered. She moaned obnoxiously the entire time she ate, telling Zack he was the king of the grill. Hannah shook her head and laughed at Lisa, "You would think he was the king of something else with the sounds you are making."

Lisa glared at Hannah, her mouth full of food so she couldn't speak. The entire table erupted in laughter. Everyone seemed to be having a good time with the exception of Brock. He sat next to Jackie and tried several times to engage her in an exclusive conversation. She only responded to him with one word answers and never met his gaze. I could tell Brock was getting nowhere with her and it was driving him crazy.

"Shall we play poker?" Hannah asked as she started to clear the plates. Jackie and I groaned, suspecting the boys would suggest strip poker which neither of us were interested in. Brock stood and took mine and Jackie's plates along with his own over to the sink. As he turned back to the group he suggested, "How about President?"

"President, I haven't played that since high school during my spare periods." Zack chuckled. Brock nodded as he returned to his seat. Lisa shrugged and pulled out three decks of cards. She handed half of them to Hannah and asked, "Any objections?"

No one said a word so the two of them started to shuffle the cards together. After a while they exchanged half of their own deck for the other's and shuffled some more. Brock smiled widely, "This is going to be fun! I miss playing this!"

Jackie shrugged, "I was never invited to play so I'm not sure I know the rules." I knew she was lying, we all knew the rules. She was just trying to get a dig in on him. Brock leaned over to his ear and whispered, "If you want, I can help you play."

She leaned away and scowled at him, "No way, you are the enemy. You will use my inexperience to your advantage!" Brock chuckled and shook his head, "I would never." Jackie let a small, involuntary smile spread across her lips before she forced it away.

It was small but both Brock and I saw it. Slowly, he was breaking down her wall. I had mixed feelings about that.

Lisa's phone buzzed on the table. She handed her half of the cards to me and answered it. As she sighed softly she announced, "Looks like Sarah is going to grace us with her presence tonight. Her plans with some guy fell through."

I chuckled and leaned forward, resting my chin on Zack's shoulder. He glanced back at me in surprise but smiled wide at the contact. It was the first time I initiated a physical connection with him in front of my friends. The moment was not lost on him, but he played it cool, only giving me a peck on the cheek before he turned his attention back to Lisa and Hannah's shuffling hands.

I whispered in Zack's ear, "Do you want to come home with me tonight?" A noticeable shiver slipped down his spine as he sighed slightly, "Always." I chuckled close to his neck and nodded. I moved away quickly and got another beer for the two of us. As I popped the top, I heard the front door slam open and a familiar voice sing, "I'm here for the party bitches!"

Lisa laughed out loud and shouted back, "Well hurry the fuck up, you are holding up the game!" Sarah giggled as she slammed the door again and came into the kitchen. She was dressed to go out in a tight red dress that was a bit high on her thigh. She had black tights on and her hair was done up in a high ponytail. Sarah pulled up a chair next to Brock and sat down.

Sarah looked around the table, her eyes fell on the two men she obviously hadn't been informed were going to be there. Zack smiled at her politely while Brock avoided meeting her eyes. She chuckled and leaned against his shoulder, "Oh Brock, no need to be so shy, you and I are very good friends." My eyes went wide and a smirk crossed my lips as I watched him uncomfortably adjust in his chair. Jackie rolled her eyes and stared at me, she mouthed 'really' to which I just shrugged.

Sarah was a free spirit. She was like a hurricane when she came through your life. She believed we were all here for a good time, not a long time and she wasn't going to be held down by social expectations of women. Sarah liked to have sex, she liked to drink and flirt, she didn't feel bad about herself either. She wasn't interested in slut shaming, all she wanted to do was live her life. Lisa and I loved her for that, she wasn't around all the time but when she was Sarah was a hoot.

Brock cleared his throat and offered Sarah an embarrassed smile, "Hey Sarah." She placed a red lipstick kiss on his cheek which caused him to blush bright crimson. Lisa laughed out loud at his predicament while Hannah stood up and offered out a round of beers. Sarah smiled and took a long sip of the cold brew, "So what are we playing here?"

"President." Hannah told her. Sarah shrugged, "I was hoping it was strip poker." I laughed out loud while Jackie groaned, obviously annoyed. Zack looked over at me with a smirk, he whispered, "Maybe later." I wiggled my eyebrows at him.

Sarah giggled as she pulled her ponytail out, "Alright, let's play!" Hannah and Lisa dealt out the cards together while we all attempted to gather them into our hands. Poor Brock kept glancing over at Jackie, while she avoided making eye contact with him at all costs. She dragged her chair closer to mine in an attempt to put some space between us.

Brock sighed heavily when he realized she wasn't happy with him. Jackie had spent time with Sarah before, but she was a bit more conservative with her views on sex. Though in my opinion it was incredibly unfair to him, in Jackie's mind Brock was tainted because he had hooked up with Sarah.

It was an incredible double standard, because Jackie never judged me for hooking up with different guys yet she judged Sarah for it. I'd broached the subject with her a few times but Jackie always dismissed it, telling me it was just different. I suspected the only reason it was different was because I was her best friend. Sarah was unapologetic with her sexual appetite; she had no qualms with being frank about herself and what she wanted. I admire that about her.

The evening passed quickly after Lisa turned on her bluetooth speaker and we started playing cards. Hours passed as cards were discarded and picked up, shuffled and redealt. As midnight approached Jackie played her last handful of cards declaring herself the president for life. She turned to me and said,

"I should go home. I've still got a few things to do early in the morning before we move my mom."

"Do you need any help with that? I have a truck and I'm free tomorrow! I can also help out on Sunday." Brock offered eagerly. He had been trying the entire night to get Jackie's attention, the desperation in his voice was evident.

She glared at him, "No, thank you very much." His face fell, Brock looked like a wounded puppy as he stood up and took the empty bottles from the table out the back door to Lisa's recycle bin. I sighed and shouted at myself in my mind as I whispered to Jackie, "I think an extra set of strong hands won't hurt."

Jackie looked at me and rolled her eyes, "He's just trying to get into my pants." I nodded, "He is, but he's also offering to help. You can let him help without letting him into your pants." Zack chuckled at my comment without looking at us. I playfully slapped his arm.

"Plus he has a truck. We can never have too many of those." I pointed out. She groaned and nodded. The rest of the table smirked at me as Brock walked back into the kitchen. Jackie stood up, without looking at him she said, "Brock, you can come and help if you want. We are meeting at my mother's house at 7am. I assume you know where it is, you knocked over our mailbox with a baseball bat four years ago."

Brock froze in his tracks as she finished telling him he could come and help. His face lit up with a smile I had never seen before. Before he could say anything, Jackie said sternly, "Don't be late." She moved around the table to collect her dish from the counter.

I took that as my cue to take her home. I smiled down at Zack, "Don't keep me waiting too long." He wiggled his eyebrows at me and whispered, "No fear. I'll take him home and be right over." We made our rounds of goodbyes before we broke apart for the evening. Sarah promised she would be there to help out, though we all suspected she would flake out as she usually did.

Jackie walked ahead of me out to the car, attempting to put as much distance between herself and Brock as possible. As I climbed into the driver's seat and started the engine she said, "I can't believe Brock Hansen is going to help me move my mother tomorrow. The universe has a weird sense of humour." I had to agree with her, the times were changing in our sleepy little town.

Chapter 20

Zack knocked on my front door about twenty minutes after I got home. I pulled him into my arms and let the door swing closed behind us. He kissed me over and over as we shuffled to my bedroom. His hands explored my body gently as I slipped my tongue into his mouth.

I moaned into his mouth and whispered, "Take off your pants cowboy." He shed his clothes in record time without breaking our kiss. I pushed him back onto my bed and climbed on top of him, I closed my hand around his erection and started to pump him lazily.

Zack's eyes glazed over as he lay back on my pillows and sighed, "Oh God, baby." I smirked as I lowered my face to his member and took him into my mouth. I heard him grunt loudly and shift his head to look down at me but I didn't look up. I took him quick and dirty, not giving Zack much time to savor. I sucked and pumped him until he exploded in my mouth. He was panting my name as he came hard.

After we were done I teased the head of his penis gently with my tongue, sending tremors up and down his spine. Zack whimpered and shook under my touch, which made me smirk. After a while I climbed up his body where I was met with a deep, passionate kiss. He cupped my face and rolled us over with him on top of me. Zack whispered against my lips, "You are amazing, baby." I giggled and shrugged.

Zack slid down my body, pausing at my jeans. He unzipped them and pulled them off, leaving me only in my cotton underwear. I realized I hadn't put on a sexy pair that night, and started to blush and covered my face. He smiled up at me as he slid my underwear down my legs slowly. Zack kissed my inner thighs and trailed up to my folds. I sucked in a deep breath as his lips came into contact with my clit.

"Layla, you are so beautiful." he whispered against my sex, I exhaled slowly as he started to lick and kiss me. I could tell he didn't have a lot of experience performing oral sex on women. He was clumsy and nervous, but I moaned loudly to assure him I was enjoying it. It took me a long time to come to orgasm but Zack was determined to get me there. When I came I let him hear me, I cried out his name and rocked my hips against his face. I could tell he was tired, but he looked up at me with a sweet smile.

Zack climbed up next to me and wrapped me up in a tight hug. I sighed and leaned into his chest. He whispered into my hair, "Sorry, I know I'm not very good at that." I shook my head, "Practice makes perfect."

He let out a loud laugh, and nodded, "Alright baby, that sounds good." After a while of laying in the afterglow Zack asked, "You are pretty good at blowjobs..."

My body went rigid at his words, I said, "Yeah, and..." He shrugged, "I was just wondering how many guys you have done this with."

I pushed him away and climbed out of my bed. Zack cleared his throat and tried to pull me back, "Layla, I don't mean it in a bad way. I'm just wondering how many partners you have had. Since we are in a relationship we should probably talk about stuff like that. I'll even go first, I have been with three women. Four if you count my highschool girlfriend who I never had sex with but we did everything else."

I stood up from the bed and pulled my top and bra off. After I put my dirty clothes in my hamper I pulled my nightgown on. I was avoiding this conversation with Zack, I didn't want to talk about it. However, he wasn't wrong, we should probably talk about it.

"Come on, Layla. This is an adult conversation and we are both adults. We should talk about it." he told me. I sighed and reluctantly nodded, Zack was right.

I ran my fingers through my hair and took a deep breath, "I have never had penetrative sex with anyone, as you know. I have had oral sex with about twenty men and hand stuff with twenty-five." Zack's eyes grew and his mouth fell open. I rolled my eyes and crossed my arms over my chest. I knew he would react that way, I could feel him judging me for my choices. I saw his face contort into disbelief before he spoke, "Are you serious?"

I nodded, "And I'm not ashamed of it. I am a healthy woman with a sexual appetite so I have acted on it. I don't advertise it because this is a small town and I don't need the entire place talking about me. I have had a lot of sex in my life and I am comfortable with it." Zack stared at me and took a deep breath, "You've got more experience then I do." That thought seemed to baffle him.

"Yes and no. I have never had penetrative sex." I reminded him. Zack shook his head, "That is a minor detail. You still have more experience. You know more about sex then I do."

I sighed, "You say that like it's a bad thing." I hissed. He shook his head quickly, "No, it's not, Layla. I just wasn't expecting it." I glared at him, "Why? Because I am fat? Because I am overweight no one would want me? Is that it?"

My tone came out harsh but I had meant it to. Zack was looking at me like it was impossible for me to have that many different men want me. He sighed, choosing his words carefully before he spoke, "I guess I didn't expect you to tell me such a high number. I'm not going to lie to you, I am shocked. I guess some of it has to do with your size but not all of it. I find you incredibly desirable so it makes sense that other men would want you the same way. I know it makes me sound like an ass, and I'm sorry for that."

He didn't give me a chance to speak before he continued, "More than anything it makes me a bit self-conscious. With that many different lovers, you would know what is good and what isn't. I wonder if I'm even in the top ten, because you would know if I was doing a good job or not. I mean it's not like you don't have options."

My anger melted away when I realized he wasn't judging me. Zack was worried he wasn't doing a good job in bed. I smiled at him and crawled up next to him on my bed, I kissed him softly and told him, "You are wonderful. I like everything you do to me. I don't compare my partners with each other, because each person is different. If it makes any sense, they are wonderful in their own way." I tried to reassure him that I wasn't comparing him to the other guys because truthfully I wasn't.

Zack chuckled, "I believe that. I just want to be the best you've ever had." I rolled my eyes and smiled softly, "Boys are so competitive."

He nodded, "We are. We all want to be the best at work, the best at kissing, the best in bed. I know it's silly and maybe a bit immature but I still want to be the best for you."

I ran my fingers through his hair and bit my lower lip. I wanted to offer him something I'd never offered to anyone else, I wanted to offer him exclusivity. I'd been thinking about it for a while. Zack was a wonderful man, I adored him and I wanted to be his and for him to be mine, just us. I smiled as I spoke, "Zack, will you be my boyfriend?"

He pulled back slightly and stared at me, "Are you serious? Because if that is a joke it's not funny." I nodded my head, "I want to be your girlfriend, exclusively and for you to be my boyfriend, exclusively. What do you say?"

Zack barely let me finish before he pulled me into a rough kiss. His arms wrapped around me as his mouth moved over mine. I moaned softly and smiled against his lips. He whispered in a husky voice, "Yes, Layla, yes." We tangled ourselves in each other's arms, wrapped up in my blankets which felt like bliss.

Chapter 21

Morning came too soon and my alarm clock woke us up at 6am. Zack groaned and rolled away from me in protest at the invasive sound. I chuckled and hit the snooze button. I told him, "I'm getting up. When it goes off again, it's up to you to turn it off."

I slowly pulled myself up from my bed and stretched my arms, shoulders and back. Zack huffed from his comfortable position, "Fine. I'll get up. Please tell me we have coffee." As I stood I nodded. His eyes were closed so I had to mutter, "Yes." Zack sighed, content with my answer.

As the coffee brewed I heard my alarm go off in the bedroom again, followed by an angry grunt and the sound of Zack's body slamming down on the mattress. I laughed to myself and called out to him, "Come on, baby, coffee will help." He groaned at me in protest from the other room. I rolled my eyes, "You promised Jackie. She will not be happy with you if you bail on her. Personally, I don't want to hear about it all day so you are going."

Zack muttered to himself as I heard him crawl out of my bed. I heard him stretch and moan, the occasional curse word slipped from his lips. I popped some bread into the toaster and shouted to him, "Come on boyfriend, I'm making you toast!"

At the mention of 'boyfriend', Zack dashed from the bedroom to the kitchen in his boxers. He crossed the distance between us, wrapped his arms around my waist and smiled down at me, "So I didn't dream that? You asked me to be your boyfriend last night?" I nodded and kissed his cheek softly, "Yes I did, and you said yes."

He lifted me up and spun me around in a circle. I giggled and wrapped my arms around his neck. Zack whispered in my ear, "What changed your mind about our relationship? I thought you didn't like labels?"

As he set me down on my feet I kissed his lips quickly, "There is something about you that I adore. I don't know how to explain it, I just want you. I've never wanted to be a girlfriend before, but with you it feels natural. It's easy with you, and I like it." Zack pulled me into a tight hug and let out a sigh. He nodded against my shoulder.

The toast popped. I moved away from him to spread the butter and put the pile of bread on a plate on the table. Zack took out two smaller plates from my cupboard and set them down for us. We ate together quietly, him smiling at me. After a few minutes Zack finally said, "I am so happy I make you feel safe. I've been trying so hard to be whatever you need me to be."

I shook my head, "I don't want you to be someone you are not. What I like the most about you is your laughter, the way you look at me. The little things are what I like the most. I love your honestly, that is the best thing about you. Don't change for me or anyone else. You are perfect as is."

Zack smiled wide at me and nodded. I hadn't meant to use the word 'love' in describing him but it had slipped out. I let it hang in the air, knowing he had caught it. We hurriedly cleaned up our breakfast and filled two travel mugs to take with us to Jackie's mom's house. Before we climbed into our separate cars, Zack kissed my forehead and muttered, "Baby, I adore you too."

Jackie was on the front lawn of her mom's house directing traffic. She had Hannah and Lisa pulling boxes from the house into their cars. A couple of guys from the Co-Op were there to help her out as well. Both of them were younger than us, but I could tell they were interested in her.

When she saw us, Jackie came racing over to Zack's truck with a large smile, "Oh wonderful, a truck! Terry and Andrew, you can bring out the bedroom suite I showed you and load it into Zack's truck here!" The two young men nodded eagerly and ran into the house as ordered. I rolled my eyes, of course Jackie would be oblivious to their interest.

I climbed out of my car and started towards the house to pick up boxes. Zack talked with Jackie for a bit to figure out where he was taking her mother's things. Some of her things were going to Jackie's but most of it was going into storage. There was no sign of Brock. Hannah and I exchanged sleepy smiles as we crossed paths. Lisa had sunglasses on to cover up her hangover. I chuckled at her slightly.

Andrew and Terry came out with a dresser, it looked very heavy. The two guys carried it with ease, both of them obviously competing to catch Jackie's eye. They brought out her mother's bedroom set in record time. When they finished Jackie looked shocked, she turned to them and said, "Wow, you guys are fast. I'm impressed." Terry smiled at her, "Anything to help you out, Jackie." Andrew frowned at him for speaking first.

"Well, I suppose Zack will have to go with this load to my place to unload. Who wants to go with him?" she asked. Zack smirked at me, he recognized the look in the young men's eyes. Terry smiled wide and smacked his friend on the back, "Andrew, you should go. I'll stay here with all the ladies."

Andrew sighed heavily and shuffled toward the passenger side of the truck. Zack pecked my lips quickly before he jumped into his truck and took off with the first furniture load. Jackie smiled at Terry, "Thank you guys for doing this for me today. It was so thoughtful. You didn't have to take the day off work for it."

"Oh of course. We love to help you out, besides it's impor- tant." Terry told her with a big smile. He reached out and touched her shoulder for a moment before letting his fingers trail down her arm. The move was lost on Jackie but I smacked the palm of my hand against my forehead softly. This guy was putting some serious moves on her and she was oblivious. Jackie just smiled sweetly at him, "Well thank you, Terry. I won't forget this."

Terry's smile grew larger as he watched her walk away back to the house. I rolled my eyes and snapped my fingers in front of his face, "Hey, Casanova, don't play all your moves in the first hour. Save some for later." His eyes shot to me as he blushed, offering a nervous nod.

We made several trips to the storage facility and Jackie's house between all of our vehicles. Her mom's house was almost empty by the time noon rolled around. Jackie had arranged for us to have sandwiches and water. She brought out a nice spread and set it on the front step for everyone. As we started to dig in Brock came barrelling up the street. He stopped short of the mailbox and jumped out of his truck. He was still in the clothes he had been in the night before. As he crossed the lawn Jackie's smile fell.

"I am so sorry I am late! I overslept and I must have turned off my alarm! SHIT!" he shouted as he approached us. Zack sighed and rubbed his forehead as Brock approached us. I could tell he was embarrassed for him. Jackie wasn't amused, instead she walked towards him and held out her hands for him to stop. Brock froze in his tracks.

She took in a deep breath before she spoke, "Just go home Brock. You obviously don't want to be here. I never wanted you here in the first place but you insisted you wanted to help and that you wouldn't let me down. It was silly of me to expect you to show up on time to actually help out. Just leave, go back home and sleep it off."

Brock's face fell, he rubbed the back of his neck nervously as he said, "I'm sorry, Jackie. I really am. I'm here now, let me help you. I want to be here." She shook her head, "No, you don't. You just want to get into my pants. Well guess what, Brock, that is NEVER going to happen so quit trying! Go home."

Hannah and Lisa sighed heavily as they watched the scene. Terry and Andrew stuffed their faces nervously with food, refusing to look up. Zack stood up and crossed the lawn to his friend's side. He whispered something I couldn't hear to Brock which seemed to only upset him more. Zack shrugged and shoved his hands into his pockets as he took a step back.

"That's not fair Jackie, I offered to help and I overslept. It's not a crime. I said I was sorry but you are acting like I'm some kind of monster. I'm not! You wouldn't be this hard on anyone else!" he huffed. Zack lifted his arms up in surrender and backed away slowly from the two of them.

Jackie glared at Brock. She took a few steps closer to him to get a closer look at him. Her eyes filled with rage as she shouted,

"Is that lipstick on your collar? Really? Really, Brock? What the hell is wrong with you?"

He rubbed his neck and looked at his hand, his face turning white. Brock began to stutter but Jackie wasn't giving him an opportunity to finish, "Just get the fuck out and stay away from me! You are such an asshole. I can't even stand you!" She stormed away from him and inside the house. Terry and Andrew looked at Brock with wide eyes as he stood there trying to gain some composure.

"I didn't do anything! Sarah showed up at my place after Zack dropped me off but I turned her down!" he shouted as the screen door of the house slammed behind Jackie. Brock brought his hands up to his head and screamed, "FUCK!!!!"

Lisa and Hannah shifted around, while I sighed heavily, "Fine. I'll deal with it." They both smiled at me sweetly, I rolled my eyes as I walked toward Brock. Zack was trying to calm him down but he was having no success. I whispered into Brock's ear, "I don't think you can salvage this, man. You need to go. All you are doing is upsetting her."

Brock sighed, "But I want to help her. This is my chance to show her I'm not a total asshole." I shook my head, "Brock, that ship has sailed for today. You aren't going to get her back. You were hours late, showed up hungover and with lipstick on your collar. You are done for the day, she's not coming back."

"I didn't sleep with Sarah, you have to believe me!" he pleaded. I nodded, "I do. I also believe you meant to be here but you overslept. Just go home, let Jackie cool down. I'll talk to her. I'm not promising anything but if you stay you will only make things worse." He nodded and reluctantly turned back toward his truck.

As Brock drove away I heard Terry and Andrew sigh. I whispered to Zack, "I think Brock might have some competition for Jackie's attention. After that little show, I'm not sure she will ever give him another chance." He nodded but didn't say anything. Zack took my hand and led me back to the front step to get some more sandwiches for lunch.

Chapter 22

After about twenty minutes I went inside the house to check on Jackie. Hannah and Lisa were arguably useless in emotionally stressful situations. They both thanked me profusely for dealing with everything. The two young men had no idea what had happened between Jackie and Brock, they both asked Zack about it as I went inside. I found Jackie in the empty kitchen looking out at the backyard. Her face was pensive, the void of any emotion. I touched her shoulder carefully as I whispered, "Hey, are you alright?"

She shrugged her shoulders, "I was foolish to expect him to show up. I knew he wouldn't. I mean, Brock Hansen wouldn't just turn over a new leaf for me right? That is preposterous. I was foolish."

I shook my head, "I don't think so. He did want to be here, Jackie. I know he did. He messed up, but Brock is the king of messing up. I know for a fact he didn't hook up with Sarah last night either. So don't let your mind go there. I know he wanted to be here to help you, it was so important to him." She rolled her eyes at my words, "Why? Why is it so important to him?"

"Because he likes you and he thought this was his shot to show you he's not a total asshole. Obviously, Brock messed that up royally but he had good intentions. I think he's liked you for a long time but didn't realize who you were. Then when he figured it out he hated himself for it because he was such a jerk to you in highschool." I told her.

Jackie turned to face me, leaning her back against the counter. She crossed her arms across her chest and sighed, "Well the damage is done. He's still an asshole and I'm not convinced he can change that." I nodded, "I completely understand. However, are you being hard on him because of his current actions or his past actions? It's important to let people evolve and grow. You and I aren't the same people we were in highschool and neither is Brock. I learned that Zack isn't the same as he used to be, and now look at us. Just remember it's important to judge him fairly."

She nodded slowly as she chewed the side of her cheek. I could tell Jackie was deciding how she was going to handle the situation. I smiled and left her to it. As I walked to the screen door I overheard Zack talking with Andrew and Terry, he seemed to be giving them advice about women.

"My best advice is to be patient. Do nice things for her, say nice things. But you have to mean them." he told them. Terry and Andrew both nodded, seeming to hang on every word Zack was telling them as though he were some sort of savant.

Terry cleared his throat before asking, "So was that guy her boyfriend?" Zack shook his head, "No, he just really wants to be. He's like you, just another guy who likes her a lot." Terry nodded, "Good, I think my gut would flip over if I found out Jackie had a boyfriend." Zack chuckled.

"That guy must have messed up really badly, because I have never seen Jackie yell at anyone like that. I've seen her stressed out, raise her voice but never yell. I was surprised to see it." Andrew muttered. Zack nodded, "Yeah, my buddy, Brock tends to bring out the worst in her. Poor bastard." Terry and Andrew laughed out loud at that.

Terry cleared his throat, "So us being here is good? She will appreciate that?" Zack smiled at the young man, "Yeah, it will go a long way."

I stepped through the screen door up behind Zack and whispered in his ear, "Are you giving these young men pick-up lines for women?" Zack pulled me into his arms and shook his head, "Nope, just some honest advice. No tricks, no lines, baby, honest." I rolled my eyes. I kissed his lips softly.

"We should keep moving. Jackie will be inside for a few minutes." I told everyone. Groans erupted from the group as people shuffled back to work. We continued to pack up various boxes and took them to the storage unit Jackie had rented. After about an hour, Brock's truck pulled up in front of the house. He sat inside it for a few moments as Zack crossed the lawn to lean through the passenger side window. They talked for a few minutes while the rest of us continued to load boxes into Zack's truck.

Jackie walked through the screen door and let it slam sofly. She peered across the lawn at Brock's truck. He climbed out of the cab when he saw her and jogged up to her. He'd showered and changed his clothes this time, thank goodness. I couldn't hear what the two of them talked about but she offered him a tentative smile and a nod. Zack wrapped his arms around my shoulders from behind and whispered in my ear, "She asked him to come back." I smiled and nodded, she was going to give him another chance.

I glanced over at Lisa and Hannah who were trying hard not to stare. Terry and Andrew watched from the tailgate of Zack's truck, both biting their bottom lips. Jackie said something to

Brock none of us could hear, but she reached out and touched his cheek softly. Brock smiled wide at her and nodded at whatever she had told him. Jackie's eyes fell back to the ground before she moved away from him and said to everyone, "We are almost done. Let's get the rest of the boxes from the back bedroom. Then we can call it a day."

Terry jogged over to Zack, his face full of concern, "What does that mean? She touched him." Zack chuckled and shrugged his shoulders, "It means you boys might be out of luck." Terry sighed heavily and nodded, turning back to the house to continue packing. I smiled to myself and whispered, "Poor boys."

Zack pulled me closer, letting his arms wrap around my hips. His breath tickled my ear as he whispered, "Exactly, they are boys. They will bounce back. I think Jackie knows the difference between a boy and a man." I shivered at his words, I nodded slightly, "I know I do." He growled slightly in my ear as his lips found my neck. I let Zack nibbled for a few moments before I patted the side of his face, "Come on, baby, let's finish up here. Then we can go home and have some fun."

Chapter 23

Jackie shouted to all of us when we arrived back at her mom's house, "Pizza and beer! Pull up some floor!". We all dashed through the screen door to the kitchen. It was surreal to see her mom's house completely empty, without a stick of furniture or a box to be seen. Jackie handed out paper plates and told us to serve ourselves. There was cold beer in the fridge.

Terry and Andrew loaded up their plates and took down entire slices of pizza in about two bites. They seemed thrilled with the concept of free beer. Brock offered to teach them to shotgun, which sent Terry over the edge in excited laughter.

Brock took a can of beer and set it down on the counter on it's side. He pulled out his pocket knife and poked a small hole in the bottom. He covered the hole with his mouth and brought the can upright, popped the tab and drank the beer down in one go. Terry and Andrew howled with excitement as they watched Brock like he was some sort of folk hero. After he finished, Brock chuckled, "See boys, it's easy."

"I want to try!" Terry cried, Andrew followed his lead. Brock set them both up, cut the small holes in the bottom and showed them how to pop the tabs. Andrew took his shotgun flawlessly, but Terry ended up coughing slightly, getting beer on his shirt. We all had a good laugh.

Jackie smiled, "Brock, you are teaching them bad habits." She shook her head, but he was undeterred, "No I'm not. This is an essential skill for young men to learn." Jackie raised her eyebrow at him and glanced at me, "Layla, shall we show him?"

I chuckled and nodded. Jackie took Brock's pocket knife and brought out two beers for us. We took our shotguns quickly and easily. Lisa and Hannah laughed loudly, "That's how it's done boys!" We giggled and shook our heads. As Jackie gave Brock his pocket knife he couldn't stop himself from staring at her with awe. He was probably trying to process how such a good girl like her knew how to do such a thing. Zack just smirked at me and wrapped his arms around my waist, he whispered, "My girlfriend is so sexy."

He kissed my cheek softly. I leaned back into Zack's embrace while he tightened his grip around me. I didn't realize I let out a soft sigh until I felt his lips curl into a smile against my cheek. He said to the rest of the crowd, "I think we are going to take off. Thanks for the pizza and beer."

Jackie smiled and crossed the room to me. She pulled me into a hug and whispered in my ear, "Thank you for all your help today." I nodded, "Of course. Anytime." Lisa and Hannah waited for their turn for a hug. Lisa chuckled in my ear and told me to 'get some', I blushed and shook my head but I couldn't stop the smile on my face.

Zack and I went to our vehicles and he followed me back to my place. We decided to take a shower, since we were both sweaty and gross from hauling boxes all day. As I stood under the hot water I let out a euphoric sigh. Zack chuckled as he removed his own clothes, "That shower must be pretty amazing, Layla."

I let the water run over my head, the water ran down my face in small rivers. As the steam filled the bathroom, Zack turned on the fan and leaned against my sink, naked. He crossed his arms over his chest and smirked at me. I knew he was watching me, I could see his interest, so I just smiled to myself and let the water do it's sensual work. I squirted some of my body wash on my lufa and soaped up my body. As the smell of mango wafted through the air, I rinsed myself off slowly. Zack stepped forward toward the shower and leaned his arms on the outside of the glass. I blew him a kiss, "Are you going to keep watching me or are you going to join?"

"I don't know baby, it's one hell of a view." he moaned as I pulled the door to the side. Zack smiled and stepped into the shower with me. I rubbed the soapy lufa all over his chest and back, which caused him to gasp. I whispered in his ear, "Yummy." I kissed across his neck, leaving wet kisses across his shoulders. Zack rested his hands against the wall and breathed heavily as I stroked his sides and continued to kiss him.

"Would you like to try something new, baby?" I asked lustfully. Zack glanced back at me, "What did you have in mind?" I raised my eyebrow and smirked, "I could give you the best orgasm of your entire life if you like. You will have to really trust me though, because I'll be giving your prostate a massage."

Zack turned around suddenly and stared down at me, his eyes wide, "My prostate? Like, in my ass? You want to go in my ass?". I shrugged, "It's up to you. I've done it before with a couple of guys, and I think you might like it. Apparently it feels so good, it's like a full body orgasm."

His face was crismon and he bit his lip slightly, "Will it hurt?" I shook my head, "No, I wouldn't hurt you. I would go slow, get you used to it. If you didn't like it, I would stop of course." Zack held his bottom lip between his teeth and nodded. I turned the water off and pulled the door back.

After we toweled off, I took Zack's hand and guided him to my bedroom. I placed a towel on my bed and laid him down on his back. He looked up at me a little unsure. I reached into my nightstand and took out my tub of lubricant. As I rubbed it over my fingertips, I whispered, "I'll go slow, sweetie, if you want to stop just tell me and I will. I promise." He nodded slowly, "Alright, I trust you."

I smiled down at him as I kissed his lips softly, "Spread your legs for me, baby. Relax as much as you can." Zack nodded. I took his penis in my hand and stroked it until he was hard. He sucked in a deep breath as I traced the outline of his anus. Zack quivered under my touch. I rubbed the lube around, slowly his puckering hole relaxed under my fingers. I stroked around in small circles for several minutes, matching the rhythm of my hand on his cock.

I took a bit more lubricant on my fingers and slowly pushed the tip of one into him. Zack's breath caught in his chest, "That feels weird." I stopped my finger and whispered, "Do you want me to stop?" He shook his head slowly. I moved my finger around inside him slightly, allowing Zack to get used to the feeling of something inside him. He sighed heavily as I tightened my grip on his shaft.

I moved my finger deeper inside Zack's hole until I was at my second knuckle. He moaned as I pulled my digit in and out of him at a slow pace. After a breathless moan, he whispered, "That feels so good, Layla." I nodded, "I know baby. I know." Once my finger was completely inside him, I searched around gently until I felt his prostate. Once I hit it, Zack arched his back slightly and bucked his hips.

I smirked as I took him into my mouth, sucking and stroking him while I massaged his prostate slowly. Zack's moans escalated to panting and soon he was writhing underneath me. I removed my lips from his cock and continued stroking him quickly until he started to shake. I smiled, knowing he was close, "Let go, Zack, let it go for me."

With a loud scream he erupted onto my hand, shooting his load over his chest. I slowed my strokes as he rode out his orgasm. Zack whimpered softly as I removed my finger from inside him. I wiped his stomach off with the edge of the towel. Once he was cleaned up, I crawled up next to him. I stretched my arms out, he rolled into my embrace and buried his face in the crook of my neck. We stayed still like that for a long time while Zack came down from his high.

"How are you feeling?" I asked him. His body was trembling against mine. Zack kissed my neck and whispered, "I can't believe how amazing that felt. I'm still shaking, baby." I giggled and nodded, "Yeah, a prostate massage can trigger a full body orgasm. I'm glad you enjoyed it." I pulled the blankets up around us when I felt Zack's breathing slow down.

After a few minutes I realized he had fallen asleep in my arms. When I tried to move away he pulled me closer. I chuckled, "Zack, I have to go clean up. I'll be right back." Zack groaned, his eyes still closed, "Fine, but hurry back."

I rolled my eyes as I washed my hands in the sink of my bathroom. I could hear Zack snoring softly. As I washed my hands I thought about what we had just done. I knew it wasn't easy for men admit they enjoyed anal stimulation but Zack seemed to handle it well. In fact, he had surrendered to me and enjoyed it completely. I looked at myself in the mirror, my face was flush and my pupils dilated. I was turned on from giving him pleasure, which I'd never experienced before. With other men, it had always been about giving something so I could get something in return. For the first time in my life, I didn't need to receive in order to feel fulfilled. With Zack, his pleasure was my pleasure.

Chapter 24

Sunday came too soon. We ended up sleeping in till noon, which I hadn't planned on. I had chores to do around my house and I needed to do laundry before the work week started. I groaned when I saw the clock and rolled over. Zack didn't move, his arm draped around my waist. I shoved it off and sat up, "It's time to get up and get moving, Zack. I have stuff to do today."

"Like what?" he mumbled, still half asleep. I stood up and stretched out my back, "Like laundry, cleaning, cooking. You know, all the stuff your mom does for you at your house." He frowned without opening his eyes. I chuckled and shook my head.

Zack groaned and hid his head under the blanket, "I don't want to get up." I went to the kitchen and made coffee, I called to him, "Well I'm not coming back to bed so you can do what you like." I took out some eggs and made a large lazy omelette while the coffee brewed. I tossed in some bacon bits, shredded cheddar cheese and green onions while the eggs cooked up. As I stirred them up, I heard Zack clear his throat and roll out of my bed. He pulled on his boxers from the night before and winced as he walked into the kitchen, the sunlight apparently too strong for his eyes.

"Coffee?" I asked. He nodded slowly as he sat down at the table. As I poured him a cup of coffee and set it down on the table in front of him. Zack didn't look up, he avoided looking at my face and stared at the table top. I raised my eyebrows slightly and retrieved the eggs from the stove. I asked him, "Do you want some?"

Zack nodded, still not looking up. I filled two plates and set one down in front of him. As I sat down and started to eat I noticed how uneasy he really was. He poked at his food but didn't eat it, he just moved it around his plate slowly. I ate my eggs quickly and washed up my plate in the sink. I finished off my coffee before I told him, "You should get going. I've got lots to do today and I'm already behind."

Zack pushed his chair back from the table and stood up quickly, "Alright, I will take the hint. I'm going." He stomped off to the bedroom to get dressed. I rolled my eyes and followed him, "What's wrong with you?" As he pulled his pants on he scowled at me, "What's wrong is you are kicking me out as fast as you can. Like I'm nothing."

I paused for a moment, "I'm not trying to be rude. I just have a lot of things I need to get done today. It's not personal." Zack scoffed as he pulled his shirt on, "After last night, it feels very personal. I let you do something to me that was incredibly personal and now you are kicking me out like I'm some one-night stand. That's cold, Layla."

"Zack, come on, I don't mean it like that." I told him. His eyes wouldn't meet mine as I tried to reach out to him. He walked past me toward my front door. I caught his hand in mine as he passed and pulled him to me, "Baby, come on. What's this about?"

He looked at the floor, his face was flush and I could tell he was upset. I tried to touch his cheek but Zack pulled away from my hand. He cleared his throat before he whispered, "I'm going to go. See you later." He pulled his hand from my grasp and rushed out my front door. I stood there, dumbfounded as the door slammed behind him. I wasn't quite sure where his outburst had come from. I wasn't trying to be rude or hurtful, I was just in a hurry to start off my Sunday chore list. Sure, I enjoyed having Zack around but he was also a distraction.

I thought about sending him a message to make sure everything was ok but before I could open the screen I got a call from Jackie. I answered, "Hey, what's up?".

"My aunt is leaving today, and home care is coming tomorrow for my mom for the first time. I am kind of nervous because I'll be at work all day while she is home with some stranger." she told me. I smiled, "I'm sure the company has strict standards for their employees. They are probably screened repeatedly before they come into a home."

Jackie was washing dishes, I could tell. I gathered up my laundry and piled it into the washing machine while she continued, "I know. She came with a bunch of reference checks. I'm just nervous because it's the first time I'm leaving my mom with a stranger. I hope they don't hate each other." I chuckled as I tossed the detergent over the clothes and turned the machine on, "Well if they do, you can try again with a different nurse."

"True. Uhh, it's just so stressful. Thank you again for yesterday. Please pass that on to Zack as well." Jackie said. I cleared my throat and whispered, "Sure, no problem.". Though honestly, I wasn't sure he wanted to hear from me for the next while. As Jackie continued to chat about her mother, my mind drifted away from Zack to my own Sunday rituals. Soon, he had slipped my mind completely.

Chapter 25

Zack's Point of View

I couldn't believe she just kicked me out of her house like I meant nothing to her. Like I was just another guy to her, nothing special. I climbed into my truck and drove home as quickly as I could. I slipped into the house, my mom had gone to church so I didn't need to face any music from her. I went to the bathroom and took a shower.

As I stood under the hot water, my mind wandered back to the night before at Layla's. The way she moved seductively under the hot spray like the most sensual exotic dancer I could ever imagine. I'd watched her, admiring the view, wanting to touch but I'd stopped myself. Layla had a lot of rules about sexual contact, it always had to be on her terms. I was fine with that, because everytime we were together it was the most euphoric experience. I'd never been with a woman who understood her body or mine as well as Layla.

As our time together continued, I became consumed with her. She always left me wanting more. I'd dated a few women in my life, most of the time they left themselves at my beck and call. My first girlfriend, Whitney, was in highschool. She was obsessed with me, and followed me around the school all the time. Whitney was beautiful but she was really insecure, she needed me to tell her I loved her all the time. To be honest, though I told her I loved her, I wasn't sure I'd ever felt it with her. Whitney was so needy, if I didn't tell her what she wanted to hear, she would break down crying.

She and I had sex for the first time in the back of my truck. After that it got way too intense for me. Whitney would come to my house and scream at my mom if I didn't call her everyday. Once she pounded on the hood of my truck during a football game until my hood shot up and wouldn't close again. Apparently I had neglected to invite her to the practice, even though no one watched them anyway. Whitney, my mom and my coach ended up having a screaming match on the football field which was so embarrassing. Brock teased me about it for years.

After Whitney, I'd dated a girl named Reba when I was twenty. She was more laid back but she wanted to move out west. Reba was fun in bed, she was wild and crazy. We never took things very seriously because she was always on her way out of town. After six months she'd saved a few thousand dollars and took off in an old Jetta to Vancouver. Reba and I had phone sex a few times but soon we fell out of touch. I didn't wish her ill or anything, we just went different ways.

I'd had a few flings over the years but I hadn't found someone I really wanted to be with until Layla. In fact, I'd been pretty taken with Layla back in highschool but she was in a different crowd then I was. Brock and I, along with our friends, had been mean to her and a few others in highschool. It wasn't because I hated her, I'd teased her because I wanted Layla to notice me. Her long strawberry blonde hair and blue eyes were beautiful against her creamy skin and rosy cheeks.

Layla's curvy body was a dream in denim. I loved to watch her sway down the halls of our school. I remember the day I knocked her into the lockers well. I'd been wanting to ask her to come to my football game but I'd chickened out and ran into her by accident. When Layla looked up at me I froze for a moment and then acted like I'd meant to. I basically ran away after that. Then I realized I wasn't going to get anywhere with her because she thought I was a dick. I was a dick, I deserved for her to view me like that. I regretted the way I treated her, I found I still regret it to this day.

When she started working at the factory I was so excited because it meant I could start over with Layla. However, she wasn't on the same line as I was and when she saw me she acted like I was invisible. Every time I got even close to having a conversation with her Brock would ruin it with a snarky comment. It took years for Layla to finally warm up enough to actually respond when I attempted to engage her in conversation.

As I stepped out of the shower I stared at myself in the mirror. I wrapped the towel around my waist and went down the hall to my bedroom. I threw myself face down on my bed and almost cried. The night before had been so intense for me. I'd never had anyone inside me before. I felt something I wasn't expecting, I'd felt vulnerable with Layla. After having the most amazing orgasm of my life I'd fallen asleep in her arms. I remembered I was trembling and my mind was swimming in euphoric sensations. Layla had taken me to a new level of intimacy and passion.

Then, the next morning, after I'd shared something with her that I'd never shared with anyone else... She kicked me out. Layla had treated me like I was some random guy she'd met at a bar. The day before she had asked me to be her boyfriend, then suddenly it was as though I was nothing.

I felt dirty and used. My pride was bruised. Maybe I was being overly sensitive, but her lack of care that morning had bothered me. All Layla wanted to do was get me out of her place so she could continue on with her day. I was suddenly inconvenient, which made me feel pathetic. I'd apologized to her, done everything on her terms, been patient with her. I had done everything right, yet still I somehow got the shaft.

I ended up doing some yard work to keep myself busy, plus it made my mom happy. As the day passed I realized Layla hadn't even texted me. She wanted her space. A part of me was heartbroken from that, because I thought we had passed that point.

My mom shouted to me that it was dinner time, I checked my watch and it was 5:32pm. Layla hadn't called me all day, just as I'd suspected she wouldn't. I locked up the shed door before I crossed the back yard toward our house. If she wanted space, I would give her space, but I was tired of it always being on her terms. I had fallen hard for Layla, and though she cared about me, it was evident that my feelings for her were stronger than hers for me. I decided I wasn't going to chase her, I was done bending over backward for her only to be pushed out into the cold.

Chapter 26

The remainder of the story will be from Layla's point of view.

I went to work on Monday expecting to find Zack waiting for me. He wasn't. His truck was in the parking lot but he had already gone into the factory by the time I arrived. At first, I didn't think much of it and just went to my locker, clocked in and started work. Maybe he had an early day.

Then lunch time came, and he didn't come down to the break room with us. Hannah, Lisa, Brock and I ate our lunch together but Zack never showed up. I asked Brock where his friend was, but he said he didn't know. I frowned at that, and sent Zack a text, asking him where he was. All I got back was 'busy', which didn't explain anything to me. I didn't see him at all for the rest of the day.

I sent him another text after supper, asking if he wanted to come over. He replied with a simple 'no, thanks', I asked why and he didn't respond. This went on for three days. I'd text Zack, he would reply that he was too busy or he didn't feel like coming over. I was getting frustrated because he wasn't even trying to talk to me.

I figured he was embarrassed about liking anal play and he didn't know how to talk about it. I thought Zack was being immature and silly so after a while I decided to just ignore him. If he wanted to talk to me like an adult, he could come and find me. Otherwise, I wasn't about to chase his silly ass all over the place. I had enough to do.

The week passed quietly at my place. Mr. Fuzz and I got our entire bed back to just ourselves. At first, I liked it. I liked the space. I enjoyed the quiet. I liked not having someone around all the time to steal the remote or eat the last helping of supper. I liked having my entire bed to myself, without someone else stealing all the covers. It was nice.

However, by the time Sunday morning rolled around I realized I missed Zack. I missed the sweet nothings he would whisper in my ears when I woke up. I missed the way he would make me laugh. I missed the way I smiled when I was with him. I wasn't unhappy by myself, I liked my alone time. I wasn't the kind of girl who needed a man to feel complete. I didn't need Zack to be happy, but I wanted him. I made myself a pot of coffee and decided I had to talk to him.

I filled a travel mug and headed over to his mom's house. She was already up and in the yard sweeping the leaves off her steps. Mrs. Trulley smiled at me as I turned off my car and opened my door. As I crossed the boulevard to the sidewalk, she called to me, "Good morning, Layla. I haven't seen you in ages! How are you?".

"I'm good, Mrs. Trulley. How are you?" I asked. She set her broom down and wiped her hands on her jeans, "Oh, I'm good. Nothing too exciting around here. The arthritis is getting pretty bad, I don't think I could keep this place if Zack didn't live with me." I cocked my head to the side. It had never occurred to me that Zack lived with his mom because she wanted him to. I'd always assumed he was just too lazy to move out because his mom did everything for him.

I took a sip of my mug, "Oh, I didn't realize you had arthritis." She chuckled, "Oh yes. It's really bad in my neck and spine. Anything I can't do upright, I can't do. It's damn annoying really." I chuckled and nodded along with her.

"So I assume you are here to see my son." Mrs. Trulley stated matter-of-factly. I felt myself blush slightly and nodded slowly. She smiled knowingly at me and told me he was in the backyard raking up the leaves. I walked around the lawn to the back fence and let myself in. I saw Zack against the fence, his back was to me. He was raking up under the fence line.

For some reason I was nervous. My stomach was full of butterflies for the first time in a long time. I swallowed hard before I called out to him, "So, you won't answer my texts with anything more than one word, so I'm here to talk." Zack spun around, wide eyed. He tightened his grip on the rake and bit his lower lip. I crossed the distance between us. When we were about four feet apart I noticed he was trying to avoid my eyes. He was nervous as well.

I rolled my eyes, "Since you are not mature enough to talk to me, I'll go first. I'm assuming you are embarrassed that you like ass play and didn't know how to handle it so you started to act all distant and childish. Well let me save you some time. No, it doesn't make you gay, a lot of guys like it and they don't like dick. I've been with a few guys who liked it, so relax." I waited for Zack to say something, but he didn't reply to me. Instead he just raised his eyes to meet mine.

"Big deal, you like to be fingered. No one cares." I muttered. He nodded and asked, "Are you done?" I frowned at him, "Well, don't you have anything to say?" Zack sighed, "Since you have me all figured out, what else is there for me to say? You've just told me how I feel so you've made up your mind."

I scoffed, "You wouldn't talk to me so what was I supposed to think?" Zack sighed heavily and set the rake down against the fence, "You could have asked me." I froze for a moment, I thought I had asked him how he felt but then I realized I hadn't.

I blinked a couple of times and muttered, "Well, you could have just told me what was going on. So tell me now."

Zack took off his work gloves and walked over to the back steps of the deck. He gestured for me to follow him. I followed him but I stayed standing in front of him with my arms crossed over my chest while he sat down. I was hovering over him, with space between us. He rested his arms casually over his knees as he spoke, "Layla, that night I shared something with you that I've never shared with anyone else. It was intense for me. I felt really vulnerable and I trusted you enough to go there. Then the next morning you kicked me out of your house like I was nothing. That's what this is about, it's not about being ashamed or embarrassed. I'm not at all, I don't think I'm gay just because I like anal play." He paused for a moment before he swallowed a ball in his throat and continued, "You keep reminding me that you've been with other guys who liked anal play, which just reminds me that I'm nothing special to you. I know for you, it's not as big of a deal but for me it meant a lot more. It's obvious to me that I have deeper feelings for you than you do for me. I mean, you kicked me out the next morning like I was some kind of one-night stand. It hurt a lot."

I sucked in a deep breath and stared at him. As his words sunk in, I thought back to that morning. I'd been annoyed at myself because I woke up late and I had a lot of things to get ready before my work week. At the time I hadn't considered that Zack had any strong feelings about what we'd done, I figured he was just excited that he'd gotten to try something wild like most guys were. It had never occurred to me that he viewed what we'd done as intimate. In my haste to get on with my day, I'd told him to leave just like I'd done every other time.

"I had no idea you felt that way." I whispered. I wasn't sure what else to say. Zack stared at me, he seemed to be waiting for me to say something else. I stared back at him for a moment, "I guess I should have been nicer to you. It won't happen again." He took in a deep breath and sighed heavily, "Baby, it happens all the time. Everything about our relationship is on your terms, none of it is on mine. I'm at your beck and call. At first I was fine with that because I wanted you to trust me but now it's like you just want me when it's convenient. I'm not a toy you can pull off the shelf and play with until you are bored with me."

I frowned at him, "I don't treat you like a toy!" Zack chuckled and shook his head, "Yes you do. You call me when you want me and kick me out when you are done with me. It's always on your terms. When you asked me to be exclusive I thought that would mean we would be more equal but after that night I realized it didn't. You treat me like an object." I rolled my eyes, "No I don't!"

"Yes, Layla, you do. And I want to mean more to you than that." Zack told me harshly. I looked away from him for a moment before I glared back at him. I didn't know what to say. I'd never had a guy talk about his feelings this much with me. Zack was expressing himself and I wasn't sure what to say. For the first time, I felt like the roles of our relationship were reversed; I was the bully and he was the overly sensitive one. Our eyes locked together as we both waited for the other to speak again.

Chapter 27

I sucked in a deep breath and shuffled my feet on the pavement beneath me. I searched his face and he searched mine, I said coldly, "So what do you want to do? Break up with me?"

Zack's eyes shot wide, "Is breaking up on the table now?" I shrugged my shoulders and lowered my eyes, "It sounds like you want to break up with me."

He sighed heavily and stood up from the steps. Zack reached out to me, he wrapped my arms around my waist and pulled my chest flush with his. He lifted my chin so I had to make eye contact with him as he whispered, "For a woman who claims to want a mature relationship, you seem uncomfortable with this mature conversation. I don't want to break up, but I want some things to change. It should be give and take, equally. Not me chasing you around, begging for a little attention."

I looked into his face and smiled slightly. I hated that he had a point. I'd made him work very hard to be with me. To be fair, he'd deserved it in the beginning. At the beginning, I didn't trust him and he had to earn it. Zack had pulled through every time, risen to every challenge. He had proven that he wanted to be with me. Now he was standing here, asking for a little credit.

"Ok." I whispered. Zack smirked at me, "Ok?" I rolled my eyes and wrapped my arms around his neck, "Ok, you have a point. I'm not used to being in relationships you know. I'm not used to someone wanting all my time and attention. It's going to take some getting used to."

Zack nodded, "I get that. I'm ok with giving you your space, baby. That's not an issue. I am not ok with being kicked out of your place after a night together." I sighed, "Ok, I'm sorry alright. I shouldn't have done that. I get it."

He chuckled, "Reluctant apology accepted." I glared playfully at him and kissed him. As I pulled away I pinched his butt and whispered, "Don't push it." Zack yelped slightly and pulled me closer. He kissed my temple and held me close. I tried not to let him notice, but as we stood close together I sucked in a deep breath. I'd missed the smell of his clothes, his shampoo, his shaving cream. His smell hit me like a tidal wave, I closed my eyes and let the aromas fill me up. I'd missed him more than I realized, at that moment I knew I was in trouble.

"Did you meet my mom?" he asked. I looked up at him and nodded, "Yeah. She, umm, told me about her arthritis. You've never mentioned that you live with her to help her out."

Zack smirked at me for a moment before he spoke, "You assumed I lived with my mom because I was too lazy to move out. I know that." I frowned and felt my face run hot, "Why didn't you tell me?" He chuckled and kissed my forehead, "I don't know. I guess I never really thought about it. I love my mom and she needs help, so the rest never really bothered me."

"I was just surprised. She told me you make it so she can stay here. That's really selfless." I told him. Zack rested his cheek against my forehead and whispered, "Well, I am a saint don't you know." I rolled my eyes and groaned while he chuckled.

"So are we all good?" I asked carefully. He peered down at me, "That depends, how are you going to make it up to me?" I could tell he was teasing; I took the bait, "Well, if your mom says it's ok for you to have a sleepover, you could come to my house for some... dessert." I felt my stomach clench at my terrible flirty words but I couldn't stop myself.

Zack's eyes widened slightly, "Hmm, that is tempting." I leaned into his chest a bit closer and said, "Maybe you could pack more than just a bag. Maybe you could have a drawer at my place, and a toothbrush in the bathroom." He pulled away slightly and forced me to look into his eyes, "Yeah? Are you sure about that?" I nodded.

I wasn't ready for Zack to have a key to my place but I was willing to let him have some space in my space. It was a compromise, and I was willing to allow him into my life. It felt strange to have a man want to be around that much. I wasn't used to it, but something told me that Zack wasn't going anywhere and a part of me was happy about that.

Chapter 28

After we had a little visit with Mrs. Trulley, Zack went to his room to pack a bag for my place. He left the two of us alone, which made me a bit nervous. His mother stared at me from across the kitchen table, an unreadable expression on her face. I shifted uncomfortably in my chair and tried to look anywhere but into her face.

"So, Layla. What are you and my son doing tonight?" Mrs. Trulley asked with a coy smirk on her face. My face flushed as my eyes shot up to look at her. I struggled to find words, my mouth lost all moisture. She seemed to enjoy watching me squirm, as I cleared my throat. Eventually I shrugged and managed a whisper, "Maybe watch a movie." She rolled her eyes and nodded. I'd never met a guy's mother before in that context. Mrs. Trulley adjusted her reading glasses and muttered, "Sure. A movie sounds fun."

It felt like Zack took forever in his bedroom. As his mother studied me sitting across from her at the table, I tried to think of something to say. I looked around the kitchen and saw a wedding photograph, I pointed at it and mumbled, "That's a beautiful picture." Mrs. Trulley turned to glance over her shoulder and nodded, "Yes, that was my wedding day. I married my high-school sweetheart Rick, that day. It was a beautiful day. We were married for fourteen years."

I vaguely remembered that Zack's father had died when we were still in highschool. I couldn't recall the details though. I could tell Mrs. Trulley was waiting for me to say something else so I blurted out, "What was the weather like?"

She laughed and shook her head, "It was warm. We got married in early September so we still had summer weather. I remember Rick was so nervous he'd sweat through his shirt before pictures so he had to change into a different one before the reception. He was so nervous, I think he thought I would change my mind right before I walked down the aisle." I smiled and nodded. Mrs. Trulley narrowed her eyes at me as she continued, "I loved that man with all my heart. Our son reminds me so much of him, so selfless and kind. He would do anything to make the people he cares about happy. Zack can be a bit naive about people's intentions, especially if they are not good."

It felt like her comment had slapped me across the face. I knew she was issuing me a warning in a not so subtle way. Mrs. Trulley's eyes didn't shift from staring at me, she let the silence fill with tension. I wasn't sure what Zack had told her about our fight so I wasn't comfortable volunteering information to her, but I wanted to offer some kind of reassurance to her. I cleared my throat and forced myself to look into her face, "I know what you mean. He is a wonderful man, I am very lucky he wants to spend time with me." She offered me a small smile and nodded.

"Ready to go baby?" Zack asked as he came back into the kitchen with an overnight duffle bag. I let out a heavy breath, relieved to no longer be alone with his mother. Mrs. Trulley stood up carefully and hugged her son. He whispered something in her ear I couldn't hear but she chuckled and nodded into his shoulder. She turned to face me and offered me a kert nod, "It was nice to see you, Layla." I held out my hand to her, she reluctantly shook it before we left.

As I climbed into my car I sighed and muttered to myself, 'Cold old witch.' I was relieved Zack was in his own truck because he couldn't hear me. I followed him to my place, replaying the abrupt conversation I'd had with his mother. I could tell she wasn't impressed with me, Mrs. Trulley probably thought I was playing with her son's heart. Perhaps, I was. I didn't have time to ponder that much since it was a short drive to my house. Zack parked on the street, leaving the driveway open for me. He pulled his bag over his shoulder and strode behind me through the front door.

Zack dropped his bag the moment the door closed behind us. He wrapped his right arm around my waist while his left hand moved my hair to the side so he could kiss my neck. I moaned softly as he trailed kisses up from the crook of my neck to behind my ear. His left arm moved around my body to completely encircle me against his chest. Zack whispered softly, "I missed you, Layla." I bit back a deep moan he nibbled on my neck.

I reached behind my head to run my fingers through his hair. Zack chuckled against my cheek and started to move forward toward my bedroom. I let him move us to the doorway. Once we were in my room I pulled my shirt off and turned around to face him. Zack smiled wide at me as I unbuttoned his flannel shirt and pushed it off. I pulled his t-shirt over his head and trailed my fingers over his pecs and down his stomach, looping my fingers into his jean pockets. I kissed him with urgency, plunging my tongue into his mouth. He groaned at my assertiveness and pulled his hands up to cup my face, deepening the kiss. I moaned into his mouth, "I've missed you too, Zack."

We tumbled into bed that night, exploring each other with sensual kisses and touching. My body seemed to call out to him in a primal way. I'd never craved a man's touch before like that, but when Zack's hands were on my skin it felt like fire and ice at the same time. It warmed me up but also sent chills down my spine. I wanted more, I craved more. We finally dozed off long after we should have gone to sleep, especially since we both worked the next morning.

When my alarm rang out in the morning I slammed it off with disgust. Zack moaned, shifting his body closer to mine. He growled into my ear, "Let's call in, baby. I'm not interested in leaving his bed." I smiled and nodded, "Yeah. Ok." We both submitted our absences through the call-in line and went back to sleep. Zack rolled over so I could be the big spoon, which made me smile wide as I let my dreams take over listening to the slow symphony of his breathing.

"Coffee." a voice whispered in the middle of a sexy dream I'd been having about Channing Tatum. I opened one eye to see Zack's sweet face staring at me with sleepy eyes. I clamped my eyes shut and squished up my face in protest. He laughed and pulled me closer, both of us still naked from the night before. Zack whispered in my ear, "We do have to get up at some point." I shook my head, pulled him on top of me, "Nope, I don't think we do."

Zack rested between my legs, his elbows up on either side of my head. He smirked down at me, "Baby, it's past eleven. I'm getting hungry." I bit my lower lip and blushed slightly as I whispered, "Eat me then." Zack's mouth dropped at my boldness. He dropped his face to my neck and started trailing his lips across my collarbone to my breasts. He traced his tongue around my nipples, sucking each one into his mouth slowly, biting down a bit before releasing to go to the other one. I gasped at the stimulation and threw my head back against my pillow. Zack moved back and forth between my breaths, trailing heated kisses and licks until I was a moaning mess under him. I panted, "Oh, Zack, I want more."

Abruptly, he moved up to my lips and kissed me hard. He wrapped his arms around my shoulders and head, pulling me as close as possible. I felt his hard penis at my entrance. I knew I was wet and ready, but before I could consent he looked down at me and smirked, "I'm afraid my hunger won't be satisfied by sexual favors. I need real sustenance. So let's go find some food."

Zack moved away from me and crawled out of my bed. The loss of contact sent a cold shiver through my body, I involuntarily grumbled at the loss of his touch. Zack looked back at me with a soft smile and wink. I rolled my eyes and sat up reluctantly, "Alright, I'm sure we can find something to eat if we must get out of bed." He laughed and pulled a pair of clean boxer shorts out of his duffle bag along with a new white t-shirt. I pulled my robe on before we headed to the kitchen.

Chapter 29

We scavenged for food in my kitchen. I'd neglected to get groceries the week before so we were left with some cheese, half a mixed fruit cup, some salami and two apples. Zack was satisfied with our make-shift meal but I was embarrassed I didn't have more to offer. We ate quietly while Mr. Fuzz walked between our legs seeking attention. He seemed to like Zack which made me happy. Mr. Fuzz wasn't a young cat, he was about ten and I had no desire to deal with someone who didn't understand how important my pet was to me. Zack rubbed his face and back with a smile and offered him a small bite of cheese which Mr. Fuzz eagerly took. I smiled, "Now he's going to beg you for food every time you are over here."

Zack shrugged, "That's fine. He and I have an understanding. We are both crazy about you so we had a little talk. He and I are going to be around for a long time so we need to get along. If I need to bribe him to gain his acceptance then so be it." I laughed at his response, "Yeah? The two of you had a discussion, did you?" Zack nodded and glanced at my cat, "Mr. Fuzz and I have a deep understanding. It's a bro-mance if you will."

I stood up to clear our plates and chuckled at him. My boyfriend and my cat were in a bro-mance. What a ridiculous concept. However, the two of them had become thick as thieves. It was adorable to watch them in their own little world. Zack picked up Mr. Fuzz and walked around the kitchen with him like a baby. No one had ever done that with my cat, including me. Somehow Zack's embrace comforted him, because Mr. Fuzz didn't fight. He just lay back and purred. I glared playfully at the two of them, "How did you get him to do that?" Zack smiled and shrugged, "I've got the magic touch." I rolled my eyes and walked to the living room to open the curtains. It turns out the first snowfall of the year was happening outside. Light fluff covered the entire yard, my car and Zack's truck. Zack walked up next to me and huffed, "Damn, my snow brush is at home."

"You can borrow mine." I offered as I watched the snowflakes fall to the ground. Zack released Mr. Fuzz and pulled me close to his chest, "Thanks sweets." I let my body nestle into his. I felt the steady rhythm of his heartbeat against my back. I was finding it harder and harder to resist his touch. I'd found myself thinking about sex with Zack more often, the actual act of loosing my virginity finally. I wondered what it would feel like to have him inside me, filling me up, throbbing and pulsing. I wondered if it would be painful or easy, would I be able to climax during my first time? I knew I'd need to figure out some form of birth control, since I'd never needed to be on it before.

"What's on your mind, baby?" Zack asked, suddenly pulling me out of my thoughts. I shook my head back to reality and blushed slightly. I cleared my throat, "Nothing, I'm just thinking about how it's about that time of year for me to get a physical." He narrowed his eyes at me and shook his head, "You are a terrible liar, Layla. Try again." Zack squeezed me tighter.

I sighed and turned around in his arms. I pulled him with me to the coach and gestured to him to sit with me. I turned my body to sit cross-legged next to him so I could fully see him. Zack searched my face, a slight frown in his eyes. I swallowed hard before I spoke just above a whisper, "I'm ready to have sex with you. I've been thinking about it a lot lately."

Zack's eyes softened, he slid as close as possible next to me on the couch. His arm wrapped around the small of my back, "Oh, baby, are you sure? Because I've been wanting this for a very long time you know." I nodded, "I know. I've been thinking about it and I'm ready. I want to have sex with you. I want your penis to be the first one inside me."

He nodded slowly, seeming to think about my words before he spoke. Carefully, Zack took my hand in his, "I think before we do this, we need to talk about what it means to both of us. So we are on the same page." I cocked my head to the side and nodded, "Alright. You go first." Zack shook his head, "No, this is your show. You go first."

I sighed and let out a flustered breath, "Fine, fine. I've never been with anyone I wanted to take that step with before. As you know, I've been saving that part of myself because I don't trust people easily. I trust you, Zack. I care about you and I want to do this with you. I think about you being inside me all the time. I know what I want and I want you." He smiled at me and nodded slowly. Zack reached up and touched my face, his voice came out husky as he said, "Ok. For me, if we have sex it means we are very serious. I know how long you have waited and I know how hard it is for you to trust and give up control. I already feel very strongly about you and I know that it's only going to intensify once we have sex. I'm probably going to fall in love with you, Layla."

"That's ok. I think I'll fall in love with you too." I told him. Zack nodded and kissed me softly. He whispered against my lips, "I might already love you, you know." I nodded. I didn't reply with words, instead I deepened our kiss. I wasn't ready to say it just yet, but I knew what I was feeling wasn't anything I'd experienced before. I could tell everything with Zack was different, it had been from the start. It felt right, it felt natural, being with Zack was like breathing. I wanted him, he wanted me, we wanted each other.

Chapter 30

I made an appointment at the Sexual Health Clinic an hour and a half away to get a physical, a pap test and discuss an IUD implant. I could have gone to the local doctor in town, but when it came to my sexual health I always went to the city. It wasn't that the doctors in town weren't good, if I had the flu or needed stitches they were fine to go to. Women's health issues were often difficult for the older doctors in town to be sensitive about. I had heard horror stories about them asking young women why they needed birth control if they were unmarried. Once I'd gone in for a pap test when I was twenty because I had been sexually active even without penile penetration, I had to explain to the doctor that I still should get checked out if I'd used various toys or fingers within my body. He tried to play it off that I was a hypochondriac which I found very ignorant.

After that, I heard about the Sexual Health Clinic in the city so I called them once to get some information. When I asked them about the pap test issue with my doctor the nurse on staff told me that I should still get a pap test. It was important to take care of my sexual health no matter what toys or body parts I used, that my concerns were valid. I made an appointment that day and I'd been going to see Cindy at the clinic ever since. She was great, she offered me lots of valuable information and whenever I had a question she made the time to take my call.

The clinic was a busy place so I had to book in two weeks from the day I called. I was a bit bummed out that I couldn't get in earlier, but I took the appointment anyway. I'd called on my break, so after I got off the phone I went to Trevor to fill out a day off request. I selected a medical appointment for the reason for the request and headed over to the slot. Trevor happened to come out of his office just as I was dropping the paper, he offered me a friendly smile and took the paper from my hand.

"Medical appointment? I hope you are alright." he said, sounding a little concerned.

I shook my head, "Everything this fine, it's just a physical." Trevor nodded, "Do you really need the whole day for that then?" I bit my lower lip before I answered, "Actually, I got to a doctor in the city. I've been going to them for years so... I have to drive."

He looked at me for a moment before he bit his lip and looked around to see if anyone was near us. Trevor reached out and touched my arm, "Come with me." I cocked my head to the side and followed him into his office. He shut the door behind us and turned to me. He ran his fingers across my arm and looked into my face, "So, I was wondering if you wanted to get a drink tonight?"

I blinked a couple of times before it sunk into my brain that Trevor was asking me out on a date. I smiled awkwardly and swallowed hard, I finally managed to say, "Sorry, but I can't. I've got a boyfriend." His face fell a little as he pulled his hand back from my arm. Trevor took a step back from me and nodded, "I see, well I guess I waited too long."

I felt my face blush slightly as I tucked my hair behind my ears. I offered him a kind smile, "I have to admit, I've always had a crush on you though, so if you had asked me a few months ago I would have said yes."

Trevor sighed and ran his fingers through his hair. He nodded and smiled, "Timing is everything isn't it?" I shrugged and moved toward the door. He cleared his throat and moved closer behind me, "If you ever find yourself single again, you should give me a call." I smiled to myself and nodded. I left his office without another word and went back to work.

All afternoon I went back and forth on whether or not I should tell Zack about Trevor. I knew he wasn't particularly possessive but since I had put sex on the table I sensed that Zack might take things a bit differently. He told me his feelings about us having sex, how in his mind it meant we were very serious. Since we were leading up to it I was afraid he would become jealous and upset. I'd always been interested in Trevor, he was handsome and funny. We got along very well, ever since I'd started working at the factory.

Zack and I had agreed to be exclusive, and I didn't want to change that. I had no intention of pursuing something with Trevor, but I still felt I should tell Zack about our conversation. I just wasn't sure how I was going to bring it up.

After work I found Zack waiting outside next to my car. I walked up to him and wrapped my arms around his neck, pulling him into a soft kiss. He seemed a bit surprised, since we were just outside of work, but he kissed me back and held on to the front of my jacket. I chuckled against his lips when his hands moved around to the back pockets of my jeans and slipped in. He whispered huskily, "Let's get you out of these tight pants and into something more comfortable."

I pushed him away slightly and nodded, letting myself smile like a childish school girl. We slipped into our separate vehicles and drove to my house. I rushed inside, Zack on my heels. He pushed me against the wall and kissed me hard. His hands moved to unbutton my jeans but I stopped them. Instead I unbuttoned his jeans and slipped them down. I maneuvered us around so his back was against the wall, then I kneeled between his legs and pulled his member out.

Slowly, I pulled him into my mouth and started to move my lips up and down. Zack sucked in a sharp breath, "Oh, fuck, Layla. That's so good." I pulled his entire length into my mouth and sucked hard, holding him in place as his hips bucked gently. I moved up and down, faster and faster as I listened to Zack's moans of ecstasy. I reached past his testes and stroked the delicate skin just behind to send him over the edge. As I stroked, I focused my attention from the head, tracing my tongue down slowly to the base and back up.

"Baby, I can't... hold it..." he cried out as he came. Zack trembled as he leaned back against the wall, completely spent. I smirked at him as I tucked his member back into his jeans. As I stood up, I said softly, "You are so sexy, baby." I kissed him softly and took a step back to admire him. He was so handsome, with toned muscles and strong arms. Even under all his clothes it was easy to make out his physique. I let my eyes trail over his body as he came down from his high before I offered him a beverage.

We sat together on my couch and talked about our day. He mentioned that he needed to head home to shovel the drive. I smiled at him as we sipped our drinks, "You are a good son." Zack shook his head, "I'm alright. Believe me she and I fight sometimes and I'm not that wonderful."

"I don't think your mother likes me very much." I confessed. He frowned at me, "What makes you say that?" I shrugged, "She wasn't very friendly to me when I came over that day to make up. Don't get me wrong, she was polite, but she didn't seem all that happy with me."

Zack smiled and nodded knowingly, "Well, I may have told her that you kicked me out of your house a few times. I was pretty upset and she asked me why, so I told her." I chewed the inside of my cheek and sighed. I suspected he had told his mother about our fight. It made sense, they were very close and he had the right to confide in someone.

"I'm a bit sad we set off on the wrong foot. I hope she won't hate me forever now." I muttered. Zack smirked at me, "She doesn't hate you. It's just that she's my mother, so she's going to be on my side. I'll talk to her, I'm sure she will warm up to you. She's just a bit over-protective."

I rolled my eyes, "Yeah, I hope you are right. Maybe I should ask her to have coffee with me sometime." Zack raised his eyebrows slightly at my suggestion but didn't say anything. I smirked, "I wanted to tell you something that happened today, but I wasn't sure exactly how to say it."

"What happened? Was it bad?" Zack asked, he reached out to take my hand in his. I smiled at him, "Not really, but I'm not sure how you are going to take it. So I wanted to find the right words. Before I tell you, I want you to know I have handled it and you don't have to worry."

He took a deep breath and nodded. I bit my bottom lip slightly before I told him, "So I booked an appointment in the city with my sexual health nurse to discuss birth control options because I don't like going to the doctors here. So I had to take the day off. Trevor asked me about it. We got to talking and he asked me to go out with him." Zack's body tensed but he held his tongue. I squeezed his hand and pulled him a little closer, he let me.

"I told him I had a boyfriend and I wasn't interested. I want to only be with you because I like the way I feel when I'm with you. I trust you, and it's important for us to always be honest with each other." I said plainly. He looked at me with wonder in his eyes, "Really?" I nodded and kissed him softly. Zack rested his hand against my cheek, his thumb ran over my lips which caused me to instinctively kiss it. He smiled and nodded, "Alright. Now it's my turn to tell you something."

I nodded, encouraging him to continue. Zack sucked in a deep breath, "I love you, Layla." I pulled him closer to me and wrapped my arms around him in a tight hug. I lifted my lips to his ear and whispered softly, "I love you too, Zack." He wrapped me up in his arms and pulled me on top of him. Before I knew it his lips were on mine and we intertwined our bodies together as our decorations sunk into our skins.

Chapter 31

By the time the weekend rolled around I was ready for it. Work had been busy with lots of overtime. Brock, Lisa, Hannah, Zack and myself had all accepted the extra work all week. The weather was getting colder, which meant the live birds couldn't sit outside as long so the killing floor was very busy. After work on Friday we all went out for beers at the bar. Jackie met up with us there, but she was a bit later because the grocery store closed around 7pm. When she walked in, still wearing her name tag, Brock's face lit up. He stood and pulled her into a hug right in front of everyone. She smiled at him and whispered something we couldn't hear.

Lisa couldn't resist and was the first to say, "Well, well, well. What do we have here?" Hannah slapped her on the arm and made a 'shh' sound but Lisa was undeterred, "Jackie, I see you are slumming it." Brock glared playfully at her as he pulled Jackie closer to his side and kissed her cheek.

"I guess I'm the good girl who fell for the bad boy. There are a ton of terrible songs about it." Jackie admitted. Lisa let out a loud whistle and ordered us all a round of shots. Zack pulled me closer to him and whispered in my ear, "That's an interesting development."

I smiled and kissed his temple, "I think you guys grew on us. You are very determined." He smirked, "Patience is the key I think." I rolled my eyes but nodded in agreement.

After a few rounds of shots and beers, I realized Lisa was acting a bit louder than usual. Hannah had tried to simmer her down but she was determined to be loud that night. At first I thought she was just blowing off steam from all the overtime we'd done but by the time she was on her seventh beer I figured it had to be something else. I glanced over at Jackie and she gave me a small nod, she recognized something was off as well. I stood up from the table and said, "Do you guys think we should get some food? I mean, we've been here for two hours, we haven't had supper."

Everyone kind of nodded and murmured in agreement. I asked Brock and Zack to go and get us some menus from the bar along with a round of nachos to share. As they left us girls alone, I leaned across the table and put my hand on top of Lisa's, "Are you alright?"

She took a long sip of her beer and narrowed her eyes at me, "Yeah, I'm great. Just great. Why?" Her voice was sharp, as though she was daring me to push her. Lisa had a tough exterior, she was like me. Sometimes she could be hard to crack but I knew there was something going on so I held her hand in place and asked again, "Lisa, what's going on? Tell us." She glared at me and yanked her hand away, "Nothing Layla, Jesus. Don't bring me down, it's Friday night, let's get hammered and have some fun."

I glanced over at Hannah who wasn't looking at any of us. She looked off to the side, letting her long brown hair hide her face. I furrowed my eyebrows and looked back at Lisa, "I know something is off so just out with it. Tell us." Lisa leaned back in her chair and stood up and yanked her hand from my grasp, "Why don't you ask Hannah." She stomped off toward the bar where Brock and Zack were standing waiting for service.

Hannah looked back at us with wide eyes. Jackie and I looked at each other, then back to Hannah. She sighed heavily and shook her head, "I don't want to talk about this here. I'm going home!" With that she stood up and stormed out of the bar in a huff. I sat back in my chair and looked over at Jackie, "What the heck was that?!"

Jackie shrugged, "I don't know. They must have had a fight or something." Brock and Zack came back with menus for all of us, Lisa had stayed at the bar to do some shots with a couple of other guys from work. I turned to look at her, she was getting so drunk way too fast. Something was very wrong, and I had no idea what had happened.

Zack leaned in and whispered in my ear, "What's up with Lisa?" I shook my head and whispered back, "I don't know, but something is really wrong."

Jackie got up and went over to the bar where Lisa was standing. She was surrounded by other co-workers of ours. Brock leaned over to Zack and I and whispered, "So I'm hoping Jackie will come home with me tonight. What do you think?" I frowned and gave him the finger, "Don't even try it, jerk. She's too smart for that."

He looked taken aback by my strong reaction, "Chill Layla. I'm only kind of serious. I know she won't go home with me yet, but I'm hoping one day." I glared at Brock and told him very quietly, "If you hurt her, I will kill you." His eyes went wide and nodded slowly. Zack chuckled, "Don't push her, man. My money's on her." Brock frowned at his friend before sitting back in his chair and sipped his beer.

"Thank you." I whispered to Zack, he squeezed my hand and nodded. I suddenly heard a loud smash and some yelling over by the bar. We spun around in time to see Lisa laying on her back in a pool of beer. She was laughing but Jackie's face held concern. She gestured for us to come over quickly, I rushed over to the scene to discover that Lisa was laying not just in beer, but shattered glass. She was far too drunk to notice but as she sat up there were small pieces of glass cutting into her back through her shirt.

"Oh God, Lisa, you are bleeding!" Jackie shreeked. I helped Lisa stand up, she was so wobbly she almost fell right back down again. Zack took her left arm, I took her right and we half carried her out to my car. Brock grabbed our jackets from the table and brought them out to the parking lot. Lisa started slurring in drunk speech, she seemed to not be very aware of her surroundings. I sighed, "I'll take her to my place. She can't be alone like this." Zack nodded, "I'll go with you, baby."

Brock looked at Jackie hopefully, "Shall we go back in?" Jackie looked between Lisa and Brock before she shook her head, "No, I think I'm going to go home. Take good care of her, guys." Jackie gave everyone a small hug before she walked over to her car. Brock sighed, his frustration was evident. I smirked at him, "Cock blocked by the drunk girl. Hilarious."

Zack laughed out loud as we put Lisa into the back seat of my car on her side, so as not to push the glass further into her back. Brock watched Jackie pull out of the parking lot before turning back to us, "Do you need my help?" I shook my head, "No, thanks though. She just needs to sleep it off." Brock walked to his truck, Zack went to his. I climbed into my car and started to drive to my place. As I turned the heat up for my drunk friend I heard her singing softly to herself a song I couldn't quite make out.

"Don't worry, Lisa. I'm going to clean you up and get you settled in on my couch." I told her. She giggled and whispered, "That's nice." I rolled my eyes and shook my head. What a disaster.

Chapter 32

I drove a little too fast to my house with Zack hot on my tail. We got Lisa out of the backseat and into my house quickly. Before we could close the door Mr. Fuzz made a run for it, slipping out between all our legs like a small ninja. I cursed and Lisa laughed. I looked at Zack and he sighed, "I'll go get him." I pulled Lisa's arm a bit tighter as he stepped away and back outside to chase after my silly cat.

"That was funny." Lisa slurred as we made our way to my bathroom. I rolled my eyes and muttered, "Yes... hilarious." I made sure she was seated on the closed toilet before I turned the lights on. Lisa wobbled a bit but she managed to stay on. I helped her spin around so her back was to me. I pulled out my first aid kit from under the sink and started going through it.

Lisa sang a Garth Brooks song softly to herself as I got the peroxide out. I moved around to stand in front of her, "Ok, Lisa, take off your shirt. Let's have a look to see how bad you cut yourself up." She continued to sing, kept her eyes closed and pulled her shirt over her head. Lisa tossed it carelessly on the floor. I examined her back, there were only a few small cuts, luckily none of them actually had shards of glass within them. I poured some of the peroxide onto a clean cloth and wiped out her wounds.

"Ouch, that hurts!" Lisa whined. I couldn't stop myself from smirking as I said, "Well, next time don't fall down on top of glass shards." She exhaled loudly, annoyed. I noticed she was looking back at me in the mirror, she seemed to be coming down from her high.

I heard Zack come back in through my front door. He was muttering to Mr. Fuzz about the importance of not running away. I chuckled to myself. I put bandaids over Lisa's deeper cuts and helped her stand up, "Wait here, I'm going to get you some pajamas." Lisa nodded slowly. She moved around to set her head down on the counter. I left her alone in the bathroom. Zack took off his jacket and crossed the room and took my hand, "Is she alright?"

I nodded, "Yeah, just some small cuts. She doesn't need stitches. I'm just getting her something to sleep in. Would you grab some blankets from the cupboard and a pillow?" He nodded. I went into my drawer, but all I had that was clean was a Christmas themed nightgown. I shrugged and brought it to her. Lisa whimpered when I tapped her on the shoulder. She sat up slowly and took the pajamas from me. I rubbed her hair playfully, "Come on. Change into that and come out. I'll get you some water and a bucket. Zack's setting up the couch for you." She nodded and ran her hand through her hair with a heavy sigh.

I left Lisa alone in the bathroom and went to the living room. Zack had set up the couch for her nicely. I found him in the kitchen giving Mr. Fuzz some wet food. He was talking to my cat as though he were a real person. I couldn't stop the smile that formed on my lips as I leaned in the doorway. Zack rubbed Mr. Fuzz's head and whispered, "You are such a suck, buddy. Also spoiled, making me chase you up and down the block. Your mom would have been devastated if I hadn't caught you. Don't do that to us again."

"Do you think he'll listen?" I asked. Zack looked up at me and shrugged, "Maybe. He seemed to love that I chased him up and down the street. If he does it again I say we let him stay outside all night. Then he will think better of it." I laughed and shook my head. I crossed the room and pulled Zack into a tight hug. I rested my head on his chest and sucked in a deep breath. He wrapped his arms around my shoulders and kissed my forehead.

I rested my hands on his hips and breathed him in slowly. Zack asked, "How is she doing?" I shrugged, "I'm not sure, I haven't made her talk about any of it. I'm going to get her some water and a bucket. Just head to bed, I'll be there in a while." He nodded and kissed me tenderly before I let him go. Zack tapped my butt softly as I passed by to the cupboard next to the sink.

Lisa groaned as she opened the bathroom door. I met her in the living room, she looked really funny in my Christmas nightgown. I crossed the room and handed her the glass of water, trying really hard not to smirk. She drank down the entire glass and muttered, "Thanks." I went back to the kitchen to refill it. When I returned Lisa had thrown herself onto the couch face down. I set the glass down on the end table and sat on the floor in front of the couch. We sat together in silence for a few minutes before I asked her, "What's going on, Lisa? You never get like you got tonight. Something is wrong, so just tell me what it is."

She whined a little before she muttered, "I don't want to talk about it, Layla." I smiled and shook my head, "Not good enough. You were bleeding in my bathroom. I patched you up and now you are sleeping it off at my house. Tell me."

Lisa huffed. I felt her move around on the couch, I glanced back to see she'd turned her back to me completely. She took a deep breath before she whispered, "Hannah and I had a really bad fight. She and I both said some things that hurt each other. Now she won't talk to me and I don't know what's going on." I nodded to myself, "What was it about?"

I felt Lisa tense up behind me, she let out a loud sigh, "She's mad at me because I love her." I chuckled slightly, "That's silly, I love her too. I also love you." Lisa groaned, "No, I actually love her, Layla. Like Zack loves you." I felt my eyes open wide, that never occurred to me. I turned around but she was still facing away from me, obviously on purpose.

"I had no idea you two were together." I said carefully. I was trying to keep my composure and not make the situation worse. Lisa had never told me she was attracted to women. We had never discussed it. I knew she rarely dated, but she was kind of private about it. Hannah dated different guys over the years, she'd had a few boyfriends. She had been adamant about men, she'd even dated Brock a little bit.

Lisa cleared her throat and sniffled a little, "We aren't, she wouldn't let me make it official. We've been best friends for years and then, one night last year it became something more. At first, we thought it was just a silly moment but then it happened again and again. We started to stay over at each other's places, go to work together, and plan dates. We were keeping it on the down-low though, because it was so out of nowhere for both of us."
I let the silence flow between us, giving Lisa lots of time to talk more if she wanted to. I knew she was drunk and hurting, the noise of the bar had been a great distraction but now that it was quiet it was harder for her to ignore how she felt.

"Then she went out with Brock and I got mad. She wasn't really interested in him but she went out with him anyway. I guess she was trying to keep the cover of being straight. Anyway, when Hannah went out with him it hurt me so I wanted to talk about it. She said it didn't matter and that Brock was just for fun." Lisa continued. I sat back and listened as she told me more, "Then, when that was done I thought she'd finally decided to be with me. Things were good for a while until I told her I wanted us to come out as a couple. I wanted her to be my girlfriend. She told me no way, that what we were doing wasn't anything serious and she didn't want to label or tie it down in any way. That was when I lost it."

I sucked in a deep breath, I asked "Then what happened?" Lisa whimpered into the back cushions before she answered, "I told her it wasn't fair to me, that I loved her and she shouldn't lead me on if she didn't feel the same way. Hannah told me I was right, that we were just friends and she didn't want to get into something else she couldn't handle. She said she didn't love me back, that she was straight and she was just curious."

"When did that happen, Lisa?" I asked her. "Last week. We've been trying to keep up appearances and go back to being friends. It was going alright until yesterday when she came to my house late and wanted to stay over. At first I was fine with it but then she kissed me. When I pulled away she said we could just have some fun together. I said no more secrets, Hannah didn't like that. Before she left she told me everything that happened between us was a mistake." Lisa told me. I turned around to look at my friend. She was curled up in a ball, still facing away from me. I reached out and touched the back of her shoulder. Lisa shivered but relaxed after a moment, "I'm sorry. That all sounds like it hurts."

Lisa sighed, I could see her nodding. I pursed my lips slightly, "You two hid it all really well. I had no idea the two of you were involved." She laughed, but it sounded sad. I watched her shake her head, "That was what Hannah wanted. I don't want to pretend anymore. The worst part is that I still love her, I love her so much." I rubbed Lisa's back softly to offer her comfort. I waited with her for a while until she was asleep and softly snoring. Zack had set a pail next to the couch for her. I went to my bedroom, he was already sound asleep. I changed quickly and crawled in next to him, wrapping my body around his.

Zack stirred slightly and leaned back into me. He didn't say anything, he just hummed. I kissed the back of his neck and whispered quietly, "Go back to sleep baby." He seemed to fall back to sleep instantly. I closed my eyes and let Zack's gentle breathing lul me to sleep. My last thought was how hard it would be to love someone who didn't love you back, to be too afraid of being with the one person who understood you the best.

Chapter 33

"Layla, I think your house guest is in the bathroom throwing up." Zack said gruffly. My eyes went wide, I had been sound asleep. When I heard Lisa's heaving through the walls I groaned and rolled away to bury my head under my pillow. He laughed at me and pulled me back against him. He whispered in my ear, "I don't think you have to get up to help her with that."

I groaned again and turned around to snuggle my face into Zack's chest. He rested his chin on the top of my head. "What time is it?" I croaked. Zack chuckled at my voice, "Like, 2am. It's not even daytime yet." I nodded and kissed his chest softly. At first I intended to fall back to sleep but he smelled so good that I kept kissing him. After a few minutes Zack's hands started to roam up and down my sides, he gripped my round butt firmly in his palms and massaged me roughly. I moaned his name as I trailed kisses up his collarbone to his neck. Zack whispered in a husky tone, "We shouldn't." I nibbled on his ear and bit down slightly, causing him to growl. I knew we shouldn't, but we wanted to. I whispered in his ear, "We will be very quiet." Zack chuckled lowly in his chest as he turned us over to he was on top of me and between my legs.

His lips found mine and locked us in a warm, tender kiss. I couldn't help it, I wanted him. I wrapped my legs tightly around his hips and reached to my bedside table. I found the condom box and pulled it onto the bed next to us. Zack looked at the box, at first not registering what it was. Then, when it sunk in he put his hand on top of it, stopping me from taking one out. I looked up at him with a frown, "We are using condoms. At least until I get my IUD." Zack shook his head, "We are not having sex tonight, Layla."

I groaned, "Why not!?" My voice came out high and whiny, I sounded like a spoiled teenager. He chuckled and shook his head, "Because your friend is throwing up in the bathroom down the hall from us. This isn't some college dorm and we are not nineteen. We can wait until it's just you and me, alone. I want it to be special for you."

"It will be special because it's with you." I whispered. Zack dipped his face into my neck and nibbled just below my earlobe. I moaned and wrapped my arms around his shoulders. His body heat was so intoxicating, I just wanted him everywhere. I reached for the condom box again but once again, Zack stopped me. I groaned and huffed, which caused him to giggle. He tossed the box back into the drawer and moved down my body until he was resting between my legs. Zack moved his fingers inside me and started to find a steady, slow rhythm which drove me crazy.

"I'm not going to fuck you right now, but I'll do the next best thing alright, baby." he told me in a husky voice that made me tremble with desire. Zack lowered his mouth to me and ran his tongue over my clit. His movements were more confident now, he knew what I liked, where to apply pressure and where to let it go. He played me like a fiddle and I was completely putty in his hands. I came really quickly, since I was so worked up. Zack teased me slightly until I flipped him over and had him under me. I pulled out my bottle of lubricant and rubbed it over my fingers.

He sucked in a tight, erotic breath as I teased his rectum with my hand. When I slid my finger into him, Zack moaned out so loudly, he had to slap his hand over his mouth to muffle the sounds. I chuckled as I took his shaft into my mouth and started to suck. He moaned my name mixed with curse words through his hands as I worked him to his peek. After he came stayed inside him a little bit longer, stroking his prostate to extend his orgasm. Zack bucked his hips and tried to hold in his cries but it was useless. I let him go and slid out, as he trembled on my bed.

We went to the bathroom to clean up afterward, but not before making sure the coast was clear. We both saw Lisa back on my couch, sleeping so we slipped down the hallway. As we washed our hands I said softly, "Why don't we spend tomorrow with your mom."

Zack made eye contact with me in the mirror, he seemed a bit surprised. As he scrubbed soap over his hands he said, "Sure, if you want." I cocked my head to the side and asked, "What?"

"Nothing, I'm just surprised you are the one wanting to make plans. It's usually me. And now, with my mother." he whispered as he rinsed his hands. I shrugged, "You are important to me. We are together and we are getting serious. It makes sense that I spend time with your mother."

He chuckled, "You want her to like you don't you?" I felt myself blush slightly and nodded, "Of course I do." Zack's eyes went wide at my admission. I took his hand and led him back to my room. We crawled back into the bed and snuggled up together. I whispered as we lay together in a cozy embrace, "I love you, Zack." He pulled me a bit closer and set his lips next to my ear, "I love you too." I closed my eyes, a relief spreading across my chest. We'd finally said it, we'd meant it. I was done pretending, I was done hiding, I wasn't pushing him away anymore.

Zack traced lazy kisses up and down my neck as I drifted off to dreamland.

Chapter 34

I was up by 7am, but I was alone in that. Zack was snoring next to me, his arm across my torso. I moved away slowly so as not to disturb him and slid out of bed. I wanted a black coffee more than I wanted anything in the world, so I closed the door behind myself and headed to the kitchen. Lisa was still sound asleep on the sofa. I checked the bucket I'd left for her and it was empty. Relief washed over me, knowing I wouldn't have to clean that up. I went to the bathroom and pulled out some Advil and set it on the counter for Lisa.

I filled my coffee maker and let it brew. As the aroma filled my house I popped some toast down. I drank my coffee and it felt like liquid rainbows after the long night with Lisa. Mr. Fuzz and I enjoyed our solitude until just before 9am when Lisa groaned and cursed from the couch, "Fuck, my back and head hurt like hell! What happened?" I laughed at her from the kitchen. I got up and poured her a cup of coffee as I called out, "Come to the kitchen. I've got pills and coffee. You will need them." She whimpered pathetically from the couch before I heard some creaking, indicating she had stood up. I heard Lisa shuffle across the carpet to the doorway of my kitchen where she peered at me through hooded eyes.

"Why does my back sting so much?" she asked. I set a cup of coffee and the Advil bottle down across from my chair and returned to my seat, "You broke a glass at the bar last night, then you fell on top of it. Don't worry, no stitches." She sank down into the chair and sighed. Lisa picked up the bottle of pills and studied them, "I don't remember much from last night. I must have drank a lot."

I let a snorted laugh escape my lips as I said, "Oh yeah, you drank way too much. Then you and Hannah had a huge fight. Hannah left. You drank more and then you fell down. Zack and I brought you here. Then you confessed all your darkest secrets." Lisa's eyes went wide with horror, "What secrets?" I smiled softly, "I don't care if you are gay, Lisa. I really don't." She almost spit out her coffee across the table at my words. Her eyes filled with tears as she whispered, "Oh no, don't tell Hannah I told you. She will never speak to me again if she knows that you know. Please, Layla, promise me." I reached across the table to comfort her, "I won't, don't worry. I will keep your secrets, but you should figure out what you are going to do."

She squeezed my hand slightly and let it go. As Lisa took another sip of her coffee she muttered, "There is nothing to do. Hannah doesn't want a relationship with a woman. She wants us to be a secret and I don't want that. I am in love with her. It's so fucked up." She tried really hard to hide her eyes but I saw the tears slide down her cheeks. I sighed and asked, "So you want to come out and she doesn't?" Lisa nodded slowly. "Well then you need to do what is best for you. I mean, not everyone is ready for the right person at the same time. Some of us need to find our own way. If she is not ready, that is ok, but that doesn't mean you can't be ready without her." I said.

Lisa stared at me for a moment before she spoke, "I love her so much, it's ridiculous. I've loved her since highschool, she's the most beautiful girl in the world but she's such a closet case. Plus she refuses to admit that we were even in a relationship. Hannah just likes to say we hung out and made each other happy. It's like we what we were together doesn't count." The hurt was evident in her voice. I could tell Lisa had let herself love Hannah deeply and then to be cast aside would have been heartbreaking. I re-filled our coffees and muttered, "You can't control her though. She's going to do things at her own pace. You need to decide what is best for you."

A groan came from my bedroom, which caused Lisa's head to snap around with wide eyes. She looked back at me and smirked, "I see he stays over the whole night now." I smiled wide and told her, "He's my boyfriend. He has his own drawer, you know." She clapped her hand over her mouth in mock shock, "Oh my goodness you hussy, what will the neighbors say?"

"They don't care, trust me." I said with a giggle. She leaned across the table and whispered, "So, how is he?" I shrugged, "I'll never kiss and tell." Lisa rolled her eyes, "Since when?" I shook my head, I'd shared various sexual exploits with my friends before but I wasn't going to share anything about Zack. Something about him was different and our sex life was just ours, it wasn't for sharing.

"Sex with Hannah was amazing..." Lisa blurted out. I choked on my coffee slightly as we both laughed. She shook her head and blushed, "Sorry, I know it's too much information but it was really good. I miss it." I wanted to ask a question but I was weary. We continued to drink our coffees, Lisa chatted about her feelings for Hannah. After a few minutes I finally got up the courage to ask her, "Is Hannah the first woman you've been with?"

Lisa smirked at me and shook her head, "No, I've had a few flings along the way. I think the reason why Hannah and I clicked so well is because we knew each other beforehand. With the others, when we got together, it was harder because the expectations were different. It hadn't evolved naturally." I smiled, "Yeah I understand. That makes sense. I mean, you know each other so well that those feelings would transfer into something physical." Lisa nodded and bit her lower lip.

"I know that Hannah is attracted to both men and women, but she only wants to be attracted to men. Whenever I brought up that I wasn't really into men, she would laugh and say 'well when I meet the right guy'; it would always make my heart sink." Lisa muttered. I nodded, "She might just need more time to figure out what she wants." My friend shook her head, "No, she's been pretty clear about it. Hannah doesn't want to go public, she doesn't want anyone to know about us. So I need to just get over it."

Lisa's eyes filled with tears again. I felt for her, I wished there was something I could say or do to make everything better but there wasn't. All I could offer was moral support and a shoulder to cry on. The relationship between Lisa and Hannah was the oldest story in the book, aside from the fact they were both women. One had stronger feelings then the other, one was more attached than the other. That's why everything is fair in love and war, I suppose.

I heard my bedroom door open along with a loud yawn. Zack had finally gotten out of bed. I smirked and called out, "Come on, baby, I've made coffee. Make sure you are decent, Lisa is still here." I heard a raspy, "Okay". Then my bedroom door closed again. I giggled and smiled at Lisa, "That means he was in his underwear when he opened the door."

She laughed loudly and sipped her coffee. After a few minutes Zack joined us in the kitchen. He had serious stubble and bedhead going, but I found his sleepy morning face to be cute. Lisa smirked at him as he crossed the kitchen, pausing behind me. Zack leaned over, wrapped his arm around my shoulders and kissed the back of my neck. It sent shivers down my spine which I could not hide. Lisa rolled her eyes and muttered, "Sure, rub it in why don't you."

"Good morning ladies." Zack muttered as he poured himself a cup of coffee. He popped some bread in the toaster and started making himself some breakfast. Lisa smirked, "Good morning

Zack Trulley. I never thought I would see this day." He chuckled and shook his head, "How are you feeling Lisa?"

She shrugged, "I'm alive. I've been better. It was pretty great of you guys to take such good care of me, so thank you both." I smiled, "No worries, Lisa. That's what friends are for." Zack nodded in agreement, not looking up from buttering his warm toast.

"I'm probably not going to get back into the drinks for a while." she told us. I rolled my eyes, "Yeah, that's probably a good idea." I was about to get up to grab another cup of coffee when my phone started to ring. I glanced at the caller ID, it read 'Hannah'. Lisa noticed it as well, her face went white. I sucked in a deep breath and answered, "Hey, how's it going?"

"Hey, how are you?" Hannah asked. I bit my lower lip and glanced over at Lisa. She was biting her thumb nail, trying not to jump up from the table. I kept my voice nonchalant, "I'm good, Zack and I are just finishing breakfast. How about you?"

Hannah cleared her throat, "I'm good. I'm just looking for Lisa. We had a bit of a misunderstanding last night and I wanted to clear the air. I went by her place this morning but she's not there. I've called but I think her phone is dead, because it's going straight to voicemail. Have you heard from her?" I looked at Lisa and handed her the phone, "It's for you."

Lisa sucked in a tight breath, "Hello?" She abruptly stood up and walked into my bedroom, closing the door behind her. Zack sat down next to me and asked, "What's that about?" I smiled at him and shrugged, "Just girl stuff."

Chapter 35

Lisa was in my bedroom for over an hour. Zack tried not to ask any questions about the night before. He called his mother to make some plans for us that day. I tidied up my kitchen while everyone else was on the phone. Mr. Fuzz and I decided to turn the television on and sit on the couch. We found some Saturday morning cartoons, Mr. Fuzz insisted his spot was on my chest, so my view was completely obstructed by his giant head. Over the years we'd had several conversations about personal space but he didn't seem to remember any of them.

Zack came in after about twenty minutes to join us. He chuckled when Mr. Fuzz made his way from my chest to his, causing me to snort, "Fairweather cat! How can you leave me like that?!"

"He just can't resist me, baby. What can I say? Don't shame him for his choices." he teased me. I crossed my arms over my chest and glared, "Oh I do shame him. For shame!" Zack laughed out loud while Mr. Fuzz just closed his eyes and snuggled in, unapologetically. I turned the television off and turned on the couch to face him.

"So, what did your mom say?" I asked carefully. He smiled softly, "She invited you over for supper tonight. She also said she was planning on doing a puzzle this afternoon if we want to join." I raised an eyebrow, a puzzle... I chuckled and shook my head, "You are kidding right?"

Zack shook his head, "Nope, my mom loves puzzles. She puts on CBC radio and will do a thousand piece puzzle in an afternoon." I was surprised that the puzzle was a planned activity for his mother. I nodded slowly, "Alright. I haven't done a puzzle in like twenty years but sure. Why not." He smirked at me and kissed my cheek, "Good, she will be pleased."

It felt so wholesome, for his mother to listen to CBC and do a puzzle on a Saturday afternoon. My parents might have done that on a weekend. I felt my stomach clench when I thought about them, it had been a long time since they'd crossed my mind. I didn't have their pictures up in my house, it had been too painful after they'd passed away to see them each day. I'd just packed everything away, pushed it down and tried to let it sink to the bottom of my psyche. With my dad, I'd only been eight so it was easier, but when my mom died, that shook me. I was twenty-two at the time. It had been her and I for so long, just like Jackie and her mom. I'd been so focused on getting through the day to day, I'd just pushed it all aside.

"Hey, Layla, are you alright?" Zack asked. I snapped back to reality with his voice. I sucked in a deep breath and looked at him. He raised an eyebrow, waiting for me to answer. I shrugged and whispered, "Sorry, I was just thinking about my mom."

He took my hand and squeezed it slightly, "You've never mentioned her before. What was she like?" I chuckled as memories flooded back in my mind. I shuffled closer to Zack as I started to tell him stories about driving in the farm truck with my parents, running through fields of canola, praying for rain and cursing the hail. I rambled on and on until I ran out of breath. He smiled the entire time, it felt good to share those memories with someone. After a while Zack pulled me closer to his chest so his arms were wrapped around my torso. Mr. Fuzz took the hint and jumped down, leaving us alone to go and search out a cozy spot to nap.

Zack kissed my neck softly, causing me to tilt my head and moan. He whispered softly into my ear, "What about your mom?" I frowned and shot him a look, "I just told you about her." He shook his head, "No, you told me about both of them. You told me mostly about your dad, what about your mom?"

I paused for a moment and thought about it. I hadn't realized, but all the stories I'd shared were about both of them. I sighed and shrugged, "I don't know. The best times we had were when my dad was still alive. After he died, my mom kind of turned inward. She didn't smile much after him. She was never the same." Zack nodded and kissed my shoulder, "My mom was the same for a long time. She didn't really come out of her shell again until she was diagnosed with arthritis. Then she kind of snapped back to reality."

I nodded, "My mom never came back really. After my dad died, she was depressed. She didn't like herself much, she focused on running the farm as best she could. Renting out the land. We moved to town and she worked part time. It was always her and I, just going through the motions."

"My mom missed my dad so much after he died. It was hard. She was like that too." he confided in me. I'd had no idea the two of us had so much in common. We'd both lost our dad's when we were younger, and our mothers had been distant and withdrawn after. It never occurred to me that Zack would understand that part of my life. Normally I didn't share that part of my life with anyone but Jackie, and we didn't talk about it much because she already knew my story. My other friends didn't really know much about it, I'd kept it private because I didn't like to share that much.

I smiled at Zack, "I wanted her to go back to the way she was before my dad died but it never happened. Then, when she got sick she went so fast. All my time was spent trying to help her and then she was gone." He nodded, "Yeah, after my dad died, my mom was the same. She went through the motions, it's common." We exchanged knowing looks and kissed softly. Every day I found something else I adored about this man. He constantly amazed me with his insights.

"I like talking to you." I stated. Zack laughed and kissed my cheek, "Well, that is good. I like talking to you too." We giggled and kissed for a little while, both of us happily ignoring the other's coffee breath. Lisa finally came out of my room with tears in her eyes. She crossed the room slowly and handed my phone back to me.

I frowned as I took my phone and set it down on the side table. Lisa sank down to the floor in front of us. Zack and I waited for her to speak but all that came from her was a loud, guttural sob. Instinctively, I reached out and pulled Lisa's shoulders into my lap. She cried as she wrapped her arms around my torso. Zack's eyes grew wide as he asked, "What happened?!"

After several deep, hard cries, Lisa managed to say, "Hannah told me she didn't appreciate that I went to her friend's house to complain about her. She is furious with me for telling you about us. She told me she doesn't want to talk to me anymore, or even see me at work." I held on to Lisa and tried to sooth her but it was no use. She was completely beside herself.

"I don't know what to do. I don't think I can fix this, Layla." she cried. I tucked her hair behind her ears and stroked it carefully. Zack sighed heavily and stared at me, mouthing to me 'What is happening?'. I shook my head and told him to 'sshh'. Zack reached for a box of tissues near the couch and set them down next to Lisa. Honestly, I think she forgot he was there. We sat together for a while, the three of us while Lisa cried her eyes out.

Chapter 36

After lunch, Lisa finally calmed down enough to go home. I dropped her off while Zack made us something to eat before we went to his mom's place. I'd helped Lisa one last time with the cuts on her back before we left my place.

As I pulled up in front of her house she turned to me with sad eyes, "Thank you for being such a good friend, Layla. You are a good person, I appreciate it." I nodded and offered her a soft smile. Before she climbed out of the car I told her, "Just give me a call if you need something." She nodded and closed the door after she stepped out. I watched Lisa cross her driveway to her front door, unlock it and go inside. I drove back to my place with an awkward smile on my face, a part of me was excited to be going home to Zack. Another part of me wasn't quite ready to process why I was excited about that.

Zack had made grilled ham and cheese sandwiches for lunch. I was so thrilled I proceeded to eat three of them. He smiled as he ate his own. It was the first time I'd pigged out in front of him and I was a little self-conscious. Zack seemed to notice my body language and shot me a heated look, "Don't you think for a second that you aren't the sexiest woman in the entire world to me. Eat as much as you want, baby."

I blushed slightly and nodded, "So, how come you used to pick on me so much about my weight?" He sighed and looked away, "I knew you would ask me that eventually." Leaning back in my chair, I smirked at him, "Well?"

"I'm not proud of it, but I went with the crowd. I always thought you were sexy as hell. I loved that you had curves, that you were round and soft. I always thought that but it wasn't accepted by the status quo. I wasn't brave enough to go against the grain and I know that's cowardly now but at the time I was a stupid kid who didn't know how to process it." he told me. I knew where he was coming from. High school was a terrible place to be different, it was hard enough to get through when you fit into the mold, nonetheless didn't.

I nodded and smiled, "So I'm sexy huh? Even when I look like a walrus?" Zack growled and shook his head. He stood up suddenly and moved around the table to pull me up so I was flush against his chest. He tangled his fingers into my hair, with his other hand he groped my hip roughly, he moaned into my ear, "You are the sexiest woman in the world, bar none. I can't get enough of you and I haven't even had the best part yet."

I chuckled and shook my head, "Walrus, remember?" Zack pulled my face to his in an intense kiss. It took my breath away. As he pulled away I whimpered slightly as he whispered in a husky voice, "More like a goddess." I couldn't help it, I enjoyed teasing him. I could feel his interest pressed against my thigh. I ran my fingertips over the back of his neck, sending shivers down his spine as I whispered, "Come now, we should get going to your mother's."

Zack groaned at my words but nodded, "Yeah, I know. Damn you got me all worked up." I winked playfully as I pulled him toward the front door. He knew I'd done it on purpose.

We drove to his mother's house in Zack's truck. He was calm but I was nervous. I had never met the mother of a boyfriend before. To be fair, I'd had a real boyfriend before either. As we parked I sucked in a deep breath silently. I was trying to compose myself. Zack shut the engine off and rubbed my leg in a comforting gesture. I glanced at him and smiled, "I'm fine." He nodded and opened the door, I followed.

His mother greeted us at the door with a pleasant smile, "Hello Layla. Nice of you to join me today. Come in, I made iced tea." I smiled and followed Mrs. Trulley into the house, Zack following behind us. She moved awkwardly through the living room and into a dining room where there was a large table with a box sitting on it. She sat down slowly in one of the chairs and groaned slightly, "Damn my hips and knees. Pisses me off." Zack shook his head with a smirk, "I'll go get us iced tea." He left to go to the kitchen, leaving me alone with his mother.

Mrs. Trulley studied me as I stood in the doorway between the living room and the dining room awkwardly. She lifted the lid from the box and showed it to me. It was a large meadow full of rainbow wildflowers, honey bees and deep blue skies. She smiled at me, "This one is two thousand pieces. Normally it would take me about a week but with you and Zack, we can do this in two afternoons." I moved through the doorway and sat at the table across from Mrs. Trulley. She dumped the pieces on the table and started to turn them all over, face up.

"I hope you like pork ribs because I got them in the slow cooker. I make my own sauce so it will be good." she told me. I joined her by flipping over the pieces and nodded. When Zack returned from the kitchen his mother reached out and held his arm, "Would you please go out and sweep the snow off my car? I'm not able to get out there on my own." He kissed the top of her head and nodded. Zack moved around behind me, leaned over and kissed the top of my head as well. As he left the room he told us, "Play nice girl."

I bit my lower lip and avoided eye contact with Mrs. Trulley. I couldn't believe she sent Zack away, the only buffer we had between us. I felt my heart rate speed up and my stomach turn over in knots. I could feel her glancing at me but I focused on turning over the puzzle pieces in front of me. After a few moments I heard her chuckle, "You know, Layla, I won't bite you."

"I know." I whispered defensively. There was an edge in my voice I hadn't intended to pass along. Mrs. Trulley smiled at me as I dared to glance up to meet her eyes. She sat back in her chair with her hands resting on the table, "Please, call me Tammy. I want you to feel comfortable here."

I smiled softly, "Alright Tammy. Thank you, I appreciate it." She nodded, "You are important to my son, so I want you and

I to get off on the right foot. He seems very taken with you, he spends time at your house overnight. I just want to be sure that you and I are on the same page." As Tammy spoke, I didn't realize I had been holding my breath. In her own friendly way, she was issuing me a warning. She wanted to make sure I had the right intentions with her son. It was the cliche parent third degree conversation as seen on television.

I swallowed hard, trying to form my words carefully, "I enjoy your son's company a lot. He is a wonderful man." Tammy's eyes didn't show any emotion as she stared at me. I bit my lower lip before I continued, "He's the first guy I've ever felt like I could trust. It's a special feeling."

Tammy nodded slowly, "Zack is a very good man, just like his father. I'm glad you see it too." With that, she started putting pieces of the puzzle together as though we hadn't just had a very awkward conversation. She was testing me, I could see it.

"I like to start with the edges first. That way we just have to fill in the middle. You can start on the flower edge, it will be easier. As a rookie, you should get the easiest job." she teased. I smirked, "Thanks, Tammy." We exchanged a friendly look before we returned to the puzzle. She still made me nervous but I could tell she was making an effort, so I knew I had to as well.

Zack returned shortly after our little talk to join the puzzle. The three of us bantered back and forth all afternoon while we drank our iced tea. The puzzle was half done by the time we ate dinner. Tammy's ribs were delicious, and I made sure to tell her more than once. Zack and I cleaned up after dinner to do all the dishes for his mom.

"Will you come back tomorrow to finish the puzzle Layla?" she asked. I smiled and nodded. Tammy stood up slowly from her chair and moved around the table until she was in front of me. She reached over and squeezed my hand softly before she whispered, "Good. Zack and you can come for brunch. I'll make a scramble." Zack whistled, "Oh mom makes the best scrambles. You are in for a treat." He pulled his mother close into a tight hug, it was the sweetest thing. It felt a bit strange to be included in someone's family time, but I had to admit, the ice tea and puzzle were quite delightful.

Chapter 37

The next two weeks went by quietly for the most part. Work was a bit slow due to colder weather. There was no overtime. Christmas was just around the corner, for the first time in a long time I had to do some real shopping. I had to get Zack a present, and I had no idea what to get him. He told me I didn't need to worry about it but I knew that was a fib. I had a sneaking suspicion he'd already picked out some things to get me and I couldn't let that go.

My appointment date came and I made the trip to the city. The roads were a bit icy but nothing I couldn't handle. I knew that trip was the perfect time to get Christmas gifts. I planned to go to my appointment first then the outlet mall on the way out of the city. Lisa and Tammy had both asked me to pick up some toilet paper for them at Costco so I made plans to go there last. I arrived at the clinic early because parking downtown was a pain in the ass. The parking cops were ruthless if you didn't plug the meter and it took me almost twenty minutes to find a spot.

I finally got into the building, signed in and waited for my turn. When Cindy came to get me she offered me a big smile, "Layla, it's nice to see you."

I followed her to the examination room where she closed the door and we sat down. I explained that I wanted an IUD as I was planning on being penetrated by my partner with his penis. Cindy smiled, she always thought it was interesting that I clarified it so much with her. Most women don't make the differentiations but I was sexually active without penile penetration. I'd been through enough embarrassing conversations with ignorant doctors before I found Cindy so I was always very clear about what my sex life involved. She had booked me in for a pap test that day which we got out of the way first. Then we discussed the options of birth control.

"Well, there are birth control pills but that means you have to take something each day or do an injection. However, it sounds like you are pretty sure about the IUD. When was the end of your last period?" Cindy asked me. I thought back for a moment, "Nine days ago." She nodded, "Alright, we are in a good spot to implant today if you want. It will become effective immediately but I would still suggest using condoms for the month just to ensure the implant took properly."

I smiled, "Alright. Let's do it." The procedure took about ten minutes, just I was still a bit tender from the pap test. Cindy was always very considerate with discomfort. She gave me several pamphlets about the IUD I'd received and told me to call her if I experienced any bleeding or discomfort. After my appointment I paid the bill and left.

I drove to the mall and staked out the shops. Early Christmas shoppers were already out and about with bags and packages in hand. I decided to start at the HomeSense store for Tammy. Though we hadn't discussed it I suspected she would buy me a gift for the holidays. We'd become closer and though she was still a bit apprehensive about me I knew she was trying. I could understand where she was coming from. In many ways, Zack was her entire support system as well as her only child. It made sense for her to want to protect him with everything she had.

There were so many random household items in HomeSense, I knew I would find something for Tammy. I settled on two one thousand piece puzzles and a warm, soft blanket. It was a very safe 'mother-in-law' gift, especially for our first Christmas together. I found a few fun pairs of socks for Jackie. She and I always exchanged funky socks for Christmas. It was a cute, inexpensive gift we would actually use. I debated getting Lisa and

Hannah anything but decided I would just give them each a bottle of alcohol instead.

All I had left was Zack, and I knew I wasn't going to find anything for him in that store. I left with my bags and went next door to Best Buy. The sales clerks were on their game that day, I had been greeted four times before I was able to make it to the back of the store. It was the season for big technology sales items. I looked around, but everything either seemed like it was too much or not enough. A tablet was way too much, he didn't need a T.V.

Finally I found some headphones and I decided to get him some Bose wireless earbuds. He could wear them at work on the floor, in the yard, when he exercised, really all the time. Zack had a pair he used all the time but they had come free with his phone and he loved those. Bose made some of the best headphones so I was sure he would jump for joy at my purchase. I left Best Buy happy with myself.

I hit up the Costco before I headed home. Zack texted me while he was on his break, sending me a very cute picture of himself in his white hard hat. He had a bit of a beard, which I had to admit looked kind of sexy. He'd told me he was going to grow one, but he had no intention to go all the way to Duck Dynasty style. Rather a groomed, snazzy style closer to this face. When Zack had told me about his plan I'd shrugged but now that I saw it in real life I found it rugged and sexy.

I send him some heart smiley faces, with the promise of some sexy time later. Zack sent me a 'lol' and a smiley face. He told me I was missed during lunch, that Hannah and Lisa still weren't sitting together or talking and it was awkward. That made me frown. I let Zack know I was hitting the road towards home, I invited him over to my place for supper.

The entire drive home I thought about Lisa and Hannah. They had been friends for a long time, before they'd become romantically involved. It made me wonder if their friendship could be salvaged. The thought of us not being able to hang out together made me sad. I knew it wasn't technically any of my business but I wondered if Hannah was sure she didn't want to give Lisa a real try. I didn't know anything about being gay, but I knew what it was like to have a secret relationship. I knew what it was like to care about someone and be afraid of what it meant. I knew what it was like to love someone and being afraid of what that meant.

Chapter 38

Zack was already at my place when I got home, I'd shown him where the hide-a-key was so he could let himself in weeks earlier. I was sure he was wondering why I hadn't made him his own copy but he never pushed it.

I found him in the kitchen with Mr. Fuzz making supper. I smiled when I saw the boiling water for spaghetti, "I invited you for supper not the other way around." Zack chuckled, "I thought I'd at least get it started. If you want to help you can."

I rushed to my storage room and set the bags in there out of sight. Zack shouted, "How was the appointment?" I returned to the kitchen and leaned against the counter, "Fine. I got the implant. It will take about a week to become completely effective. But after that we are good to go for unprotected sex."

Zack's eyes went wide, "I've never had sex without a condom." It was as though a lightbulb went off in his head with that statement. He turned to me for a moment, still processing and I couldn't help but giggled a little. Zack smirked at me and turned back to the pot of water. He broke apart the spaghetti noodles and tossed them in.

"Are you sure you don't want to use condoms?" he asked. I shrugged, "Well I don't have any STI's and you have never had unprotected sex so we don't really need them as long as we are exclusive. If you are worried about it, we can." He shook his head vigorously, "No, no I don't want to use them. What guy would? I'm just surprised it's on the table that's all."

I shrugged, "Well why would we? I mean, we aren't kids. We aren't worried about pregnancy. STI's aren't a concern. We are monogamous. So why wouldn't it be on the table?" He moved toward me and wrapped his arms around my waist, "I don't know. I just wasn't expecting it. Every girlfriend I've ever had wanted to use them. So it's what I'm used to."

I nodded, "That makes sense. I've heard bareback sex is better for the guy then condoms. I've done some research and apparently everything feels more intense. You can feel the blood flow, the moisture, the trembling. Apparently it's really sexy and makes quite a difference." Zack's back shivered as I spoke, "Layla, baby, you are setting me all worked up." I giggled and ran my fingers down his spine.

I whispered softly in his ear, "I'm a bit tender today with the pap test and implant. But if you are feeling frisky I can do some things for you." His lips found my neck as he nibbled and kissed his way up to my lips. Zack's whiskers were smoother than I'd expected, they didn't feel harsh against my skin. I kissed him back eagerly and slipped my tongue into his mouth.

"Supper first." he whispered against my lips. I could tell it was taking all of his strength to step back from me to stir the noodles. I smirked to myself and opened up the pasta sauce to head it up on the stove in a pot. I noticed Zack ran his fingers through his hair a few times, as though he was trying to calm himself down. I smirked to myself.

"So how else was the city?" he finally asked as we sat down to eat. I shrugged, "I got my Christmas shopping done. I think your mom will like what I got her. I got socks for Jackie." Zack smiled as he started to eat, "It's sweet that you got my mom something. Did you get me something?"

I shrugged, "I guess you'll have to see." He chuckled at my teasing. "I'm just going to get Lisa and Hannah a bottle of alcohol each from the liquor store." He nodded, "That's what Brock and I do every year, but it's a case of beer."

Before I could say anything Zack sat back against his chair, "Those two are so dramatic," I frowned, "Which two?" Zack sighed, "Lisa and Hannah. If one is sitting at the table with us the other won't sit down. Then one of them will stomp off and sit alone in the break room. It sucks, they won't just talk it out." I nodded but didn't say anything. Zack sighed, annoyed, "Like today, Lisa was sitting with us at lunch. Hannah sat as far away as possible from our table and glared at her the entire time. When I went to sit with her, trying to make her feel better she told me that Lisa and her were not speaking and that she had no intention of ever sitting with her again. What am I supposed to say? It was just so much drama."

I shook my head, "Yeah they just need to talk it out. To be honest I'm not sure they will be able to fix it though. I mean, they are both still really mad and it's been weeks." Zack huffed loudly, "Well it shouldn't be like this. They are going to have to get over it."

"You don't know anything about women do you?" I asked, teasing. Zack smirked at me, "I know a little bit about you. I think that counts." I rolled my eyes but couldn't stop from smiling. "I am not like a lot of girls, Zack. I'm not sure being with me will prepare you for much of anything." I reminded him. He shook his head, "That's the best thing about you, I love that you aren't like most girls. I love you just the way you are."

He stood up from the table, taking our plates to the sink. He pulled my hands, making me rise from my chair. Zack pulled my arms around his neck, moving his hands down to rest on my hips. He swayed us back and forth, slow dancing to a song playing in his head. I chuckled but snuggled my face into his neck and breathed deeply. He whispered, "See, this is why. This moment right here." I nodded but stayed silent, enjoying the innocence of our embrace.

"I love you, Layla. I'm not going to stop loving you. I've always loved you, even when I was too much of a coward to admit it to myself." he told me. I pulled back slightly so I could see his face. Zack smiled down at me, his eyes were focused and serious. I smiled, "I know, I love you too." He pulled me closer, "I'm going to spend the rest of my life showing you what my love is. I promise."

My breath hitched in my chest as his words, I bit my lower lip as I whispered, "Don't make promises like that, Zack. You can't know that." He shook his head, "I do know. I've known since high school." I felt my eyes grow misty, my voice trembled as I spoke, "Don't ask me yet. I'm not ready."

Zack pulled my head into the crook of his neck, he chuckled, "I know you aren't, baby. I won't yet, but I am telling you that I will. I will wait for you to be ready." I could feel my body shake in his arms, an odd combination of relief and fear coursing through me. No one had ever promised me anything that big before. It was foreign, like out of a story book.

Slowly, I took his hand and silently gestured for him to follow me. I pulled him to my bedroom where we took each other's clothes off without a single word. As we wrapped up in each other's arms I let his words sink into my mind, my heart and my soul with his warm lips on my skin.

Chapter 39

I decided to host a small gathering at my house the week before Christmas for all our friends. It was a Saturday afternoon and my kitchen was a bustle of activity. Zack had insisted on cooking a turkey, but neither of us had never made one so we were kind of winging it. He had left the lid off of the bird too early so the outside was brown but the inside wasn't fully cooked. Zack was frustrated, "The damn thing will be black by the time the inside is cooked."

"Cover it up with this. It will be alright. Dull side out I think." I told him, handing the roll of tinfoil. He nodded and wrapped up his precious bird. I smiled to myself. I stirred the boiling potatoes, they were almost ready for mashing. Zack pushed the roaster back into the oven and turned to get another pot from my cupboard, "Stove Top!" I smiled and passed him the two boxes.

A knock hit my door and Zack shooed me out of the kitchen. I chuckled as I turned the knob to see Brock and Jackie. They had arrived together, his arm around her shoulders. I smiled, "Come in guys. Get a drink. Zack is trying to save his bird." I heard a loud grunt from the kitchen, followed by my boyfriend's voice, "I have saved it! You will see!"

"He's cooking? Really? Does he know how to cook?" Brock asked as they walked in. I shrugged, "I guess we will see." Jackie giggled. She produced a small package which made me smile wide. I turned to my small tree and grabbed the package with her name on it. Jackie and I opened up our gifts at the same time while Brock went to the kitchen to get them some drinks.

Jackie had given me two pairs of socks. One was white with rainbow unicorns on them. The other was navy blue with green alien spaceships. I shrieked with excitement. She did the same and we hugged each other. She whispered in my ear, "I love them." I nodded and told her thank you. Jackie and I sat down on the couch, she leaned in to whisper, "Are Lisa and Hannah coming?" I nodded.

Her body went rigid, "Oh, Layla this might be bad." I frowned, "Why?" Jackie looked back toward the kitchen before she whispered, "Lisa told me she has been seeing Sarah for a little while. What if she brings her here?"

I shrugged, "Hannah was the one who didn't want to be official. Lisa gave her the option for them to be together and Hannah refused. So she has no recourse for it." Jackie shot me a look, "It's not that simple. Hannah cares about Lisa, she's just not ready."

"I know but she can't expect Lisa to wait around for her. Especially when they want different things right now. Hannah can do what she likes, but so can Lisa." I reminded her. Jackie rolled her eyes, "You know how Hannah feels about Sarah." I nodded, "I know. You feel the same way. Sarah owns herself, I like that about her." Jackie frowned but didn't say anything.

"Besides, I invited Sarah on her own anyway because she is my friend. So she might be here anyway." I told her. Jackie's eyes went wide, "Oh shit." I laughed out loud.

Brock came back with three beers, one for each of us. He smiled softly at Jackie, "Are you girls talking about me?" Jackie shook her head, "No, actually. Not a thing about you." He pouted, "Oh, well I'll have to try harder then I guess." I chuckled and held my bottle of beer out to him, "Here's to you, making my best friend happy."

He froze for a moment before he clinked the necks of our bottles together. Jackie kissed his cheek while Brock tried to find words to say. Luckily for him a knock hit my door so I stood up to answer it.

Hannah arrived with a bottle of Jack Daniels for me. I handed her the bottle bag I'd gotten for her. She smiled and gave me a quick hug, "Merry Christmas everyone!" She joined Jackie and Brock on the couch while I went to the kitchen to get her a beer. Zack smiled when I walked up behind him and patted his butt.

"Hey baby, supper is almost ready." he told me. I nodded and started to get the plates out of the cupboard. He'd mashed the potatoes and the carrots were ready along with the stuffing. Zack pulled the turkey out of the oven and was letting it rest before carving into it. After a few minutes I called our friends to get their supper. Everyone came in with huge smiles on their faces. Zack received all kinds of compliments on his bird, which caused him to smirk and puff out his chest with pride.

From the kitchen I heard a loud sing-song voice, "Hello! Merry Christmas!" I recognized Sarah, "In here! We are just getting food." She walked in with Lisa trailing behind. Hannah's face fell into a tight, unreadable expression. Brock smiled but Jackie glared at him, causing him to look down. The friendly excitement in my kitchen fell into uncomfortable silence.

"Come on in, grab a plate and eat some of my masterpiece." Zack suggested to them with a smile. I patted his shoulder, silently thanking him for being his wonderful self. Lisa nodded awkwardly, while Sarah was oblivious to the tension in the room. We all ate, and slowly over time the energy went back to normal. Laughter and smiles replaced uncomfortable fidgeting.

Hannah couldn't keep her eyes off of Lisa and Sarah though. After a while, it became obvious to me that she was jealous.

At one point, Sarah leaned over and rubbed Lisa's knee and it looked like Hannah was going to crawl across the floor to snap her neck. If Lisa noticed she was oblivious to it all. She talked with everyone as though nothing was amiss. When it was time for dessert Sarah and I went to the kitchen with everyone's plates.

I started to pull the pudding parfaits out of the fridge. I had made vanilla and chocolate pudding, layered it and put hazelnuts on top. Sarah was impressed, "Wow, you are like Martha Stewart." I shook my head, "No, that would be Zack. I just made instant pudding." Sarah and I got the desserts ready and brought them out to everyone. It appeared our supper had been a success, I whispered in Zack's ear, "This was a great idea." He smiled and kissed my forehead.

Lisa and Sarah offered to do the dishes for us. I got them all set up in the kitchen. Hannah insisted on drying. Jackie shot me a look, so I stayed in the kitchen to ensure nothing escalated too quickly. I busied myself with packing up left overs while small talk filled the room. Lisa washed while Sarah rinsed and Hannah dried. It was awkward to watch.

"Don't splash me babe, I don't want dishwater all over my dress." Sarah teased. Lisa smirked and playfully splashed at her again. Hannah glared at them before setting a plate down on the counter a little too loudly. Sarah glanced over at her and asked, "You ok?"

Hannah frowned, "I'm great. So how long have you two been a thing?" Sarah's eyes went wide before she glanced back at Lisa. She carefully handed another plate to Hannah as she said, "Oh, not long. We are just having some fun, right Lisa?" Lisa nodded smuggly. Hannah took the plate and dried it quickly before she set it down on top of the other one loudly.

"I didn't know you were into girls." Hannah hissed at Sarah. I raised my eyebrows. I had a bad feeling this conversation wasn't going to a good place. Sarah giggled, "I have dated both men and women." Hannah nodded, crossing her arms over her chest, "So you will basically just sleep with anything? As long as it's got a pulse?" Lisa sucked in a harsh breath.

"Hannah, that's not fair." I told her, coming to Sarah's defence. I knew many of the people in town thought Sarah was loose, but I didn't believe in slut-shaming. I liked Sarah as a person, even if she was a bit flaky. She didn't deserve such judgement, no one did. Hannah glared at me, "Isn't it? I'm not saying anything that isn't true."

Sarah offered a soft smile, "If it makes you feel better to say that about me, then go ahead. It's nothing I haven't heard before. It doesn't hurt me like you want it to." Lisa wrapped her arm around Sarah's shoulders, "She knows what she likes and what she wants. And that's sexy as fuck." Hannah's eyes met Lisa's. They exchanged looks before Hannah muttered, "What kind of a future is there with someone like her?"

Lisa shrugged, "I am not sure. But she doesn't make me hide in the closet. She holds my hand when we are out together." Sarah looked back and forth between the two of them before she gasped softly, "Is Hannah the girl you were with before?" Lisa nodded and turned back to the sink, avoiding eye contact with anyone.

Sarah turned back to Hannah and offered her a soft smile, "I didn't realize. I'm sorry if it seemed like I was trying to rub it in your face. Lisa wouldn't tell me your name, she didn't want to betray your trust." Hannah stepped back and threw the tea towel she'd been holding hard against the counter. She stomped out of the kitchen like an angry toddler. I heard my front door slam, which sent Jackie rushing into the kitchen asking, "What the hell happened?!"

"I didn't know. Lisa didn't tell me." Sarah told her, her face pensive. Jackie nodded slowly as she leaned next to me against the counter. Lisa refused to turn around, she continued to wash the dishes vigorously until there was nothing left on the counter. Sarah and I resumed the rinsing and drying as the silence drifted around the room.

Sarah was the one to finally break it. She held onto Lisa's hand tightly and forced her to make eye contact, "You should go after her." Lisa frowned at her and shook her head, "Why? I came here with you." Sarah smiled and nodded, "I know but you love her, and she loves you. We both know this. You should go get her." Jackie smiled, a small tear slid down her cheek but she wiped it away swiftly. I nodded slowly. Lisa looked at both of us before going back to Sarah, "But that's not fair to you."

She shrugged and smiled, "It's not about what's fair. You love her, I can tell. Don't let her go. Go on Lisa, go get her." Lisa kissed her cheek softly before turning to me, "Can I borrow your car?" I nodded and grabbed my keys from my purse. Lisa threw her jacket on and rushed out the door after Hannah. Jackie cried out excitedly and jumped up and down. She gave Sarah a quick hug, which neither was expecting before she returned to the living room in search of Brock.

I pulled Sarah into a hug. We didn't say anything for a moment, I just held her. I felt her wipe her eyes slightly before she stepped back and smiled, "I hope that works out for them." I nodded and told her, "You are an amazing person, you know. Don't forget that." She sighed and flipped her hair, "Oh I know." We chuckled and returned to the living room. Zack had found Miracle on 34th Street on T.V. We all curled up and watched the movie, pausing only to make hot chocolate with Bailey's half way through.

Chapter 40

It was midnight, Christmas Eve when it finally happened. I slipped out of my nightgown and left it next to the bed. Zack smiled at me as I beckoned him to the bed with my index finger. He shed all his clothes and met my lips first before the rest of our bodies tumbled together. I let myself fall back onto my bed, pulling his body with mine. Zack rested his upper body on his arms so as not to crush me. He kissed me and explored my mouth with his tongue, causing me to moan.

He pulled back for a moment and stared down at me, "Hello beautiful." I smiled and pulled his lips back to mine and I tangled my fingers into his hair. Zack positioned himself so his erection was at my entrance and slowly stroked me up and down. I was already very excited, I moved my hips to encourage him to enter me. He rested his forehead against mine, sucking in deep breaths as he eased himself inside. My breath hitched in my throat, I'd never felt so full in my entire life.

Nothing I had done before compared to the feeling of Zack inside me. I felt his breath on my skin as his hips rocked against mine. His member throbbed inside me, my insides trembled with excitement and desire for more. I wrapped my legs around his hips, trying to make him rock deeper. His movements sent shivers up and down my skin, everywhere.

"So soft, I can feel everything. You are my own personal heaven." he whispered, breathing hard into my ear. I moaned and nodded. I could feel his heartbeat against my chest as his breathing became more laboured. As we worked toward our ecstasy I lost myself in my feelings for him. Zack kissed me, pulled me as close as possible. He sent me over the edge with a loud whimper. Zack thrust gently a few more times until he shook and stilled his movements inside me. We continued to kiss as we came down. Our first official time together had been just like they say it is in the movies, which made me chuckle inwardly to myself.

"So, what do you think?" I asked playfully. Zack looked down at me and smirked, "I think we are going to do it again." I giggled uncontrollably as he flipped us around so I was on top. We made love over and over again late into the night.

The next morning we went to his mother's house early to make breakfast with her and open gifts. Tammy got me a sweater, some new socks and a gift certificate to get the oil changed in my car. I couldn't help but smile at the traditional 'parent gifts' she'd given me. She was thrilled with the puzzles, especially when I told her Zack and I would do them with her on Sundays.

I handed Zack his incredibly small package and he raised his eyebrows, "Did you get me a ring here, baby?" I rolled my eyes and told him to just open it. When he saw the earbuds he smiled wide, "Oh yeah! This is so awesome, baby! Thank you!" I reached into my pocket and handed him his other gift, "This is also for you. Something you can use everyday." Zack opened his hand and nodded. When he looked up at me his eyes were a little misty but he blinked it away. Zack took his keys from his pockets and slid the key to my house onto the chain. Tammy smiled softly, but pretended not to notice.

Zack pulled out a big bag from behind the Christmas tree with my name on it. I took out the tissue paper from the top and peeked inside. He'd gotten me a new, wool lined denim jacket. It was so nice and warm. I was so excited. There were some socks in the bag as well as another small bag inside that read, 'Mr. Fuzz'. I opened it up, Zack had bought him two bags of his favorite cat treats.

I pulled Zack into a hug and kissed him passionately. His mother chuckled, I felt Zack blush against my face. I smirked at him when I let him go. He cleared his throat before he announced, "Breakfast!"

Zack made us all eggs benedict with hashbrowns and toast for the three of us. Tammy was thrilled that Zack was becoming such a good cook. She told me he had never cooked until he met me. Zack shook his head, in an attempt to deny it but I smiled knowingly.

We'd been invited for Christmas supper at Jackie's. At 3pm the three of us got into my car and headed over. Brock was outside shoveling the walk way when we arrived. It was obvious he was making sure Tammy wouldn't fall, which I thought was very considerate. Zack helped his mother into the house while I went straight to the kitchen to give Jackie a hand. The guys stayed in the living room with the mothers, out of the way.

"Merry Christmas!" Hannah's voice rang through the house from the front door. I crossed the kitchen, down the hall to the living room to see Lisa and Hannah walk through the door. Lisa helped Hannah take off her coat and hung it up in the front entry closet. I moved up to Hannah and wrapped her up in a hug. She returned it.

I whispered into her ear, "Merry Christmas, Hannah." She didn't say anything but as we pulled apart Lisa took her hand and kissed it affectionately. Hannah smiled at her and leaned her head against Lisa's shoulder. It was the sweetest moment.

"Layla, don't you dare leave me alone! Why does it look like that?!" Jackie shouted from the kitchen. The living room erupted in laughter as I rushed back to the kitchen, hoping I wasn't entering a disaster zone. Luckily Jackie was just confused about why the stuffing was coming out of the bird. We hadn't laced it up tight enough. After we fixed it, Jackie sighed, "Stupid bird." I chuckled and nodded, "My feelings exactly."

THE END